All that & everything

Books by Karen Turner:
All That & Everything

Broughton Hall series:
Torn
Inviolate
Stormbird

All that & everything

Karen Turner

Published by Karen Turner

First published 2009

Reprinted 2021

Cover and text designed by Simon Sherry for Palmer Higgs
Cover painting by Liliana Vacis Murua
Typesetting by Palmer Higgs

ISBN: 978 0 646 51976 0

www.karenturner.com.au

For Dad

About the author

Karen Turner was born in Melbourne, Australia. After leaving school, she commenced a career spanning more than twenty years in the Financial Services Industry which presented the opportunity to work in Singapore, Hong Kong, New Zealand, and Australia.

Throughout this time, Karen managed to indulge her first love - music - and over the years performed with inumerable bands, and participated in many musical productions and functions.

As an escape from the intensity of the corporate world, Karen discovered a passion for fictional prose which led to this, her first book, a rather eclectic compilation of award-winning short stories - All That & Everything.

Karen's first novel, Torn, was quickly followed by its sequel, Inviolate. Her latest book, Stormbird, was released in April 2019.

Karen lives with her husband Stuart, and her cats Panda and Katie, in Victoria's beautiful Riverina region.

When she's not hammering away at her computer, she likes keeping fit and catching up with friends.

Contents

A book by any other cover

You can tell a lot about someone by the shoes they wear.

Every morning, the 4:30 city bound train pulls away from Frankston station like a rumbly, fat caterpillar. On board is a handful of sleep deprived passengers, commuting and committed at this ungodly hour.

Give or take one or two ring-ins, the core group was the same each morning. Alice knows them by their preferred footwear. It's not really a shoe fixation, not like the usual thing people get for shoes, the way they can buy two or three pairs in a single outing. This is more observation.

Alice fancies she knows these people intimately; where they are going, what their jobs are, even what they earn. It's one of those things you do on a train when you don't read or listen to music. You daydream and make things up. She knows their names and families and social lives. All because of the shoes they wear.

Take George, for example. She'd named him George after the fat teddy bear she had when she was small. George the teddy had vacant button eyes and a benign grin, just like George the commuter.

She glances at him now. George wears the black leather slip-ons with the non-slip sole. They have little tassels on the tops that have begun to curl with age. He carries a weathered black Gladstone bag filled with Encyclopedias – on compact disk – for sale. He's never used a computer in his life, but his customers don't know that. He talks the talk and is fluent in download, ram, disk-space *et al*.

George earns the basic wage but that's okay by George because his mother died a few years ago and left him the house. He's always the first into the carriage, and predictably, sits in the same seat, just inside the door, where he maintains a one-sided conversation all the way to his stop, which is Cheltenham.

Marilyn, named for her white-blonde hair, teased and sprayed to within an inch of its life, teeters on four inch patent leathers. Today they're black to match the black and white hounds-tooth suit she wears. Yesterday they were red, complementing her navy and red suit.

She approaches a seat, examines it carefully, touches any suspicious stains and brushes off dust and crumbs with a tissue from her patent handbag before finally conferring approval by sitting on it.

Marilyn's an employment consultant, but if you asked her she'd say she was *in HR*. Human Resources, wasn't that where you go to buy a new foot if your old one was worn out? She'd like you to think she was on a huge salary but reality is, recruitment's not too hot at the moment and she's on commission. She checks her lipstick twice, reapplying once, before getting off at Flagstaff Station.

She'll be heading straight to the office to get a few hours uninterrupted time in, before meeting the girls at Joe's for a skinny latte.

Jack works in a furniture factory. His battered Blundstones have drips of varnish on them that make them look permanently wet. His wife hates him working in that place because one of Jack's workmates had this accident with a machine last year. But Jack's on good money, better than some of the guys at footy training last night, so he thinks the risk is worth it. He tells the missus he's careful but never gives workplace safety a thought when he alights at Moorabbin.

Brett rides his pushy straight up to the door, hops off and lifts it into the carriage. He hangs it by its handle bars over the railing inside the door, right in front of George. George sniffs and tucks his slip-ons further under his seat even though Brett's bike is nowhere near them.

Brett sits by the window, stretches his chicken legs out before him, and studies his grotty runners. They smell to high heaven from being out in all weathers but when you're a courier, riding the deadly-treadly around the city streets all day, you've gotta be comfy and despite their holes, these runners are his favorites. Their laces hardly tie up anymore, so frayed are they, but Brett never cares about that. He just tucks their scruffy ends out of the way into the tops of the shoes.

Brett's head bobs up and down in time with the dull doof-doof faintly audible from his headphones. He closes his eyes and crosses his legs at the ankles, one sneaker over the other. He's settling in, going all the way to Flinders Street. He's happy with the freedom of his job. It doesn't pay a lot, but then, it would, if he didn't knock off at lunch time. He just couldn't be stuffed with this full-time work thing; as long as he gets enough to pay the rent and chip in for his share of the dope every weekend.

Each morning Jason stands by the open door having a last drag on his smoke before the announcement – *Flinders Street train stopping all stations to Flinders Street via the City Loop now departing, stand clear please, stand clear.* Jason is a tradey, still doing his apprenticeship for a builder on one of those new housing sites. He gets off the train in Mordialloc and his boss picks him up in the work van on the way through. When the wind is blowing from the wrong direction you can catch a whiff of his smoke inside the train.

Jason grinds his cigarette butt out under his mud-caked work boots and hikes his backpack higher onto his shoulder. Marilyn's nose wrinkles distastefully as Jason trails dried mud across the floor to his seat. He likes to have the three in a row all to himself and he sits in the middle, backpack next to him on the window side. He scrambles inside and pulls out a tatty biker magazine.

Alice has watched Jason pore over that magazine for a week now and is almost looking forward to the day he can afford to buy the red Kawasaki as much as he is.

Alice turns to the doors expectantly. Frederik isn't here yet. The one person she catches this crappy train at this ridiculous hour for. Frederik should be royal, hence the name she has bestowed. His shoes are polished, Italian leather from the sole to the upper. His suits are wool, dark conservative colours, sometimes pin-striped, sometimes not. His shirts are crisp and always white, and his ties are silk. His white-gold tie clip matches his cuff-links.

Frederik is a successful lawyer, unmarried because his work keeps him too busy. He's been with a girl for a couple of months but is going to have to let her down gently because he doesn't think it's fair on her given his work commitments.

The station guard blows the whistle and there's a shout. Frederik bursts into the carriage, dragging his laptop computer in its custom-made bag in after him, just as the doors begin to close. He's uncharacteristically flustered, and self conscious as all eyes, even Brett's, swivel his way. The doors slide together and he takes the nearest seat – right next to Alice!

He'd never sat next to Alice before. His fragrance drifts to her and it's as warm and spicy as she'd always wanted it to be. Her heart is beating so strongly she can see her blouse moving. She clasps her hands together on her lap to still their agitation.

The train pulls away from Frankston station, rocking and bouncing its passengers in time with each other like some strange, jerky dance.

Alice looks down. Her glance takes in her own shoes. Would someone wearing Italian leathers be interested in someone wearing vinyl courts?

Doubt it.

Jason drools over his magazine, Marilyn flicks through her filofax, George mutters under his breath to himself, and Brett changes the CD in his player. Alice stares out the window, trancelike, but aware of Frederik in every nerve, every cell, in her body.

She focuses on her breathing in an attempt to control her excitement. Frederik. He was sitting right beside her!

Without warning, the train bucks, its brakes screeching their protest. Jason looks up, his brow furrowed while Jack curses softly. Marilyn makes a tutting sound and continues her flicking, George asks himself what the problem is and Brett drops his CD. It frisbees across the gritty lino floor and ends up at Frederik's polished toe.

The train is at a standstill when Brett comes over to claim the CD from Frederik, the distinctive reek of aged sneaker drifts from him.

"I think it's all scratched," Frederik offers.

"Ta," Brett says, examining it. "Yeah, looks pretty rooted. Was my fave too."

Frederik smiles politely.

Brett was about to return to his seat when the train had some sort of convulsion. Jolted off his feet, he lands *plop* onto Marilyn's filofax complete with her up-turned hand.

"Eeugh!" She gasps in horror, her fastidious nose catching his scent.

Brett yelps in surprise, "Geez lady, I don't even know ya." Marilyn tries to tug her hand free from where it cups the well worn seat of Brett's jeans but suddenly the carriage jolts again and he is flung further off balance, his full weight now on her lap, his sweat-stained T-shirt pressed against her spotless suit jacket.

"Get off me!" Marilyn cries indignantly, pushing at him with her free hand. The train continues its jerky bunny-hop, and Marilyn fails to maintain her composure. While her hand is trapped under the bottom of a smelly, unsavory youth, her fellow travelers watch with various degrees of enjoyment.

Alice pinches her lips together to keep from laughing and she can feel Frederik tensing with suppressed mirth beside her.

Jason chuckles out loud and George describes to himself what just happened.

The train seems to settle for a moment. Marilyn's face is beetroot with outrage and disgust. Taking advantage of the lull in the movement, she musters her strength and gives an almighty shove with her free hand.

Just as she pushes all her weight into the middle of Brett's back, the train jerks the opposite way and Brett falls forward onto the floor, Marilyn's momentum takes her with him.

The two fall to the floor and that's when Alice can restrain herself no longer. Thankfully her laughter is drowned by Marilyn's furious cries and Brett's protests of virtue.

Frederik leaps over to offer Marilyn his hand but though she grasps it, he is weakened by hilarity and can't do much to help. The backwards joggling of the carriage continues to throw them all off balance, and Frederik can do no more than hang onto the support pole with one hand and Marilyn's hand with the other.

Static hisses and a voice announces over the intercom that the train is faulty and will be returning to Frankston Station.

"No shit," responds Jack and George explains the announcement to himself.

Brett manages to scramble out from under Marilyn. He tries to assist Frederik in helping Marilyn to her feet but she slaps his hand away.

Frederik's and Brett's eyes meet, glassy with tears, over Marilyn's coiffure. Frederik helps her back to her seat, the height of her heels hindering her progress as the train continues limping into Frankston.

Now, Brett makes his way back to his seat, after all that, the CD is still triumphantly in his hand.

Frederik returns to his seat, and catches Alice watching him. He smiles sharing the moment. "Well, that kicks the day off nicely."

She smiles in return. "I wonder how long we'll be delayed."

"No idea." He really looked at her then and she felt very self-conscious under his green gaze. "You catch this train every morning don't you?"

She nods, flushing and tongue-tied.

"Will you be late to work?"

"No, not really." She searches her mind for something amusing, something interesting, something … anything to say that will hold his interest.

Marilyn sits opposite dusting her suit and checking her hair and make-up in her compact. As soon as the train arrives at Frankston and the electronic doors release, she is out of her seat and clip-clopping resentfully down the platform.

Jack figures he can still make the bus, his Blundstones squelch past her.

"Will you be late?" Alice asks. *Boy that was clever.* They get to their feet and stand back to let Brett unhook his bike from the hand rail.

Frederik sighs. "No. That's one of the benefits of being your own boss."

His own boss? Of a law firm?

"What do you do?" She asks bravely.

"I'm a software salesman," he replies. He pats his computer bag affectionately. "It's all in here. Remember encyclopedias? Well this is new, it's all online and does a lot more than your old conventional book type of thing. All you need's a computer and away you go."

Alice's mouth forms an O and she unwittingly shoots a glance at George as he pushes past Brett and steps out onto the platform.

"Anyway," Frederik is saying, "I'm not *that* into it that I'll hassle people on the train. But I do like to catch the early one to get into the office and do a bit of paperwork before chasing down new business."

They step out into the morning half-light. It's hard to believe that only 10 minutes has passed. Alice feels as though half a day has gone by already.

"So what about you?" He asks. "What do you do?"

"I'm a veterinary assistant," she replies shyly.

"Oh?" They walk side by side toward the ticket office. "So how come you get in so early?"

Here's the good bit, she thinks. *Do I tell him I have no life or what?*

"I don't have to, it's just that I like to get in early so I can check on the overnight patients and clean their cages out and everything."

"It's still an early train for that isn't it?"

"Oh, I'm an early riser," she says breezily, leaving out the bit about being early to bed too.

They arrive at the ticket counter just as Jason finishes talking to the man in the booth.

"Train's gonna be delayed a while," he says. "Fifteen minutes or so."

"Thanks," Frederik says.

Jason shrugs. "Better go ring the hospital, tell 'em I'll be late." He disappears down the ramp to the public phones.

Frederik turns to Alice. "Wouldn't pick him for a nurse, would you?"

"A nurse? What about the workboots?"

"Lives on a farm. I sat next to him the other day and he was telling me. He gets changed when he gets to work." Frederik shakes his head. "Everyone's got a story to tell haven't they?" he observes cheerfully. Suddenly he turns to her and smiles, "Hey, how about a coffee, and you can tell me yours." He holds out his hand, "I'm Sam, by the way."

The small town

It was just a small town, and they all loved him, but not as much as Becky. He was everything she could want in a man; strong yet kind, with a quick smile and a cheerful word.

He was a real *do-er* too, always out in the yard, splitting logs to keep the house warm, weeding and planting in the garden, and picking the fat, green grubs off the cabbages, while she lay beneath a tree, her adoring brown eyes following his every move.

Hour after hour, she watched him at his back-breaking work, in his floppy hat and worn overalls with a T-shirt underneath, his pale arms and neck turning pink in the sun. At intervals, he straightened, rubbed the small of his back, and wiped the sweat from his forehead with his hat.

Eventually, he would glance across to her and say, "Not long now, Beck. Nearly done, then we'll go in and have cuppa, eh?"

At night, they ate their evening meal together, and he would read to her from the newspaper. Sometimes she sat on the floor between his knees and he would brush her hair until it shone like a mirror.

He was so gentle with her, and patient with her inability to be more than she was, for he loved her in return. Theirs was the perfect relationship and they both knew it, and everyone in the small town knew it too.

Every Friday morning, they left their white, weather-board house on the outskirts of Rosewood, to tramp the five miles of unmade road into town. Jack Lloyd dragged behind him a home-made cart, filled as high as he could manage, with vegetables from the garden to sell or exchange, for meat, milk, eggs, flour, and just about anything else he could barter.

In the rain, they left two lanes of footprints and a set of cart-tracks through the mud, and in the sun they left a haze of dust behind them.

He talked all the way, telling her of his hopes; his plans for a better paying job, a bigger house, with a grand garden – one you could sit in, not just for growing vegies – with a picket fence, and a race for chooks up the back. And all his sentences were prefaced, *when this damn war is over*.

He said she was pretty, and she was, with her glossy black hair and expressive brown eyes that could shine with happiness, or soften with love, like warm chocolate.

He was her opposite. Where she was dark, he was light, the night and the day, two halves of the one. She didn't know what she thought of his looks, to her it was all quite irrelevant. She knew only that he was much taller than she, and that she loved him beyond all else.

Becky listened as he talked, and she hung on every word, for she loved his voice, its resonance and its depth. Her heart lifted to its sound, and as they walked she cocked her head up to look at him, and his head tilted down.

This particular Friday, the summer sun beat down on them as they walked. Jack's fair skin was shaded by his floppy hat, but still his nose was burning. Becky's dark head attracted the sun, and touching her hair, he said, "Not too hot?" She smiled and kept walking, content to be beside him and unconcerned by the heat.

As they walked, the paddocks and orchards gave way to houses; whitewashed weather-board places like their own, but unlike theirs, the houses closer to town didn't have furrows of leafy vegetables, blushing tomatoes and capsicums, stands of corn or runs of beans. These gardens were generally unkempt, weedy spaces with woody azaleas and dead-headed rose bushes. The men in these houses worked either at Stanton's vast sheep stations to the east of town in the foothills of the Dividing Range, or in the woollen mills to the north.

The wheels of Jack's cart moved easier as the road closer to town was in better repair. When finally the unsealed track became bitumen, they knew they were nearly there. As the glorious scent of freshly baked bread drifted over from Finlay's Bakery, they crossed the railway line and found themselves on the main street amongst the bustling Friday morning community.

Everyone in Rosewood knew Jack for he'd lived here all his life. His father still ran the post office and lived in the flat upstairs, just like he always had. As Jack and Becky made their way toward Angelo's Fresh Fruits and Vegetables, Ernest Watkins called out from across the street, "G'day Jack, G'day Becky," and Jack responded with his friendly salute and Becky with her smile.

Mrs. Adams was sweeping the porch outside her cafe, her face ruddy and damp with effort. She pulled a hanky from the pocket of her pinny and dabbed at her brow as they drew even with her. "You an' Becky come in for a cuppa later eh, Jack?" she said, grateful of the opportunity to break from her work. "Bill Stanton reckons he wanted to see ya 'bout a job in the shearin' shed, but since ya got no phone, said to tell ya he'll be in at eleven."

Jack nodded. "Okay," he said. "Me an' Beck just gotta sort this stuff out an' we'll be in."

Red-haired, identical twin Simpson boys were riding identical blue pushbikes along the side of the road, each holding an empty jam-jar. The one Jack thought might be Bert yelled out, "Hey Jack, you mind if we take a short-cut through your place to the creek?"

The one that must be Davie added, "We're after taddies."

"Nah, you're right, just mind you don't tread on me baby carrots," Jack shouted with a laugh, and he and Becky stopped at Angelo's. Becky stood apart as Jack dragged the loaded cart to the side of the footpath. Pushing open the door, the bell jangled cheerily and Jack hung back to let Becky go in first.

Becky loved Angelo's Fresh Fruits and Vegetables. The shop was always clean and welcoming and smelled of fresh vegetables and herbs. Angelo's wife, a spherical lady with limited English, always had a cool drink for each of them and a plate of homemade *biscotti* for Jack and Becky to share.

"*Eh, bella ragazza, bella ragazza,*" Senora Palmisano said as Becky happily attended to her biscuit.

Jack grinned proudly, "Can say that again missus, she's beautiful all right." Angelo Palmisano appeared from the back of the shop, wiping his hands down the front of his apron. "*Ciao* Jack, *ciao* Becky," he said, his round face splitting in a broad grin. "What did you bring me today?"

A short time later, a wad of cash in his pocket and the last biscuit crumbs brushed from his fingers, Jack held the door for Becky and they emerged from the shop, back out into the mid-morning summer sun.

Next stop was the post office to pick up their mail. James Lloyd, tall like his son, was adding figures on a notepad when they entered. He had his head down, showing the bald spot on his crown, and Jack saw how his father's yellow hair had faded to white, and knew he was looking at his own image thirty years hence. The older man's glasses had slid to the end of his nose and he pushed them back with a finger as he looked up.

James loved Becky like she was his own. He welcomed her enthusiastically and she returned his greeting. When James looked to his son, his welcome was tempered by a small crease that formed between his brows, and his mouth was turned down.

"What is it, Dad?" Jack asked.

Becky heard the flat note in Jack's voice and quieted immediately.

Wordlessly, James went to the back table to retrieve his son's mail. Jack flicked through the usual assortment of bills, letters, and advertising material until an envelope, heavy with import, singled itself out by its bold, type-written face.

Flipping the envelope over, Jack read the return address and very slowly, he raised his head. Young blue eyes met faded older ones, and he said, "It's from the War Office."

James nodded and touched his son's arm, "It's your turn son, they're callin' you up."

Jack and Becky didn't go to Mrs. Adams' café. Instead, they went straight home, each lost in their own thoughts, heads down, eyes unseeing, and feet trudging automatically along the well-worn road.

Two days later, the whole town was there at the station. Marion and Shirley from the Railway Hotel were attempting a tuneless but gay version of *Don't Sit Under the Apple Tree*, while little Gordy Wheeler kept time on his drum, and the Simpson twins *plunka-plunka'd* on their banjos. Mrs. Adams handed Jack a bag of freshly ground coffee beans, and Senora Palmisano thrust a box of *biscotti* at him.

Bill Stanton had let the boys have the afternoon off seeing as how Rosewood's favourite son was going to war. The shops had all shut their doors for the afternoon as the crowd gathered on the platform and the children ran around firing toy guns at each other.

No-one in this whole world could have been as proud as Becky that day, and though her heart was breaking, she gave no outward sign of it. Her man was going to war, they said, to secure his country's freedom. But she didn't care for the reason, she cared only for his return; a day so distant, it didn't have a date. In a vortex of sound, excitement, and emotion, she stood in its quiet eye, and before them all, he kissed her brow and promised to love her forever.

As the train hissed and spewed steam and cinders over the crowd, the choir from Saint Anthony's started up a rendition of *Waltzing Matilda*. The women flapped their hankies and the men waved their hats, and the children cheered and ran alongside the train until the platform ended – and then, he was gone.

———

James took Becky home to his flat over the post office, and tried not to think of Jack's garden going to ruin on the edge of town.

Each day before James went downstairs to open the post

office, he looked to where Becky lay listlessly in her bed. "It's okay," he said, "he'll be home one day."

The sight of her brown velvet eyes, raised to his in mute pain, haunted his day but he could find no relief, for he too grieved, and he too feared.

As the months passed, the summer slipped away and winter fiercely made its presence felt. James pulled a chair close to the fire and Becky rarely moved from it – even to eat. Her once glossy, black hair hung limp, uncared for and dull, and her weight-loss was plain.

When letters arrived, James brought them upstairs from the post office. They saved them for the cold evenings when there was nothing better to do than stare miserably at each other. James would open the envelope and smooth out the pages of slow writing, before reading them out loud.

During the reading, Becky stared at nothing, and when James was finished, she closed her eyes, shuttering out the world, and retreating into her private sorrow.

Winter turned to spring and the trees, newly clothed in glorious blossom, hummed with bees. James did not think at all about Jack's garden, though he wondered if Becky did.

———

When the telegram arrived from the War Office, James shut the post office door and placed the CLOSED sign in the window. With his elbows on the counter and his head in his hands, he wept for the loss of his son until he thought his heart would stop.

Such waste; such folly of man.

Long after it had grown dark, he climbed the steps, a weary old man, much older now than he'd been that morning when he'd descended. He didn't know how he was going to say the words to her.

They brought him home to lay him down, but there was no fanfare, there was no welcoming committee. James stood on the platform alone but for Robert Henry the undertaker, waiting for the train to arrive.

And it rained.

James thought it was as if all the angels in Heaven were weeping with him, sluicing his tears away with their own. James and Robert slid the wooden box from the freight car and Robert, his hand on James' shoulder, said, "Don't you worry now Jim, I'll take care of things from here."

———

Rosewood's cemetery was flanked on one side by a stream that bubbled happily in spring but dried up to a sullen trickle by the end of summer. On the other side was a paddock inhabited by a flock of bored sheep. It took only one to wander over to the fence before the rest decided to follow. They watched the gathering of townspeople, all standing around a single opening in the ground, then disinterestedly, they returned to their grazing.

The sound of hushed weeping washed beneath the words Father Patrick intoned over the gravesite. Jack had loved this town and all who lived here, so James had symbolically chosen rosewood for his son's coffin.

Becky stood beside James, her head bowed in silent grief. When the service ended, the people came over to pay their respects to the pair – a hug, a pat on the back for James, a touch, a whispered word for Becky – and then, they drifted away.

Marion and Shirley were holding the wake at the Railway Hotel, and as the cemetery workers packed up their shovels and followed the rest of the town, James looked to Becky. "Shall we go, lass?" he said.

She raised stricken eyes to his in wordless communication, and he bowed his head. Slowly turning, he walked away, a bent, solitary figure.

Alone with her one love, Becky sat beside his earthy bed, and with her head resting on the freshly dug mound, she breathed deeply of the pungent, loamy smell, and exhaled a heart-wrenching howl that raised the heads of the sheep next-door.

As the days passed, no amount of coaxing could remove the dog from the grave. The townspeople brought food, but it went untouched, and finally, a year to the day since Jack had kissed her goodbye, Becky found her peace.

The townspeople of Rosewood decided a break in tradition was the only course of action. They dug into Jack's grave and placed a second, much smaller, rosewood coffin atop his own. Jack's headstone told how he had died in action. Now, the stonemason added four extra words:

Becky, died of love.

Note Inspired by a poem by Robert Skepper – *Until He Returns*

The river-gum

As the woman turns onto the dirt road, her car raises a wake of summered dust behind her. She stares in disappointment, balking at the non-descript brick veneers with their designer-kids and Austar satellite dishes, for despite the unexpected reality of all-conquering suburbia, her mind's eye still recalls the paddocks of gently lowing cattle, yellowed grassy fields, sloping folds of earth, and the blue-green forests of her childhood.

Caught in the hamster-wheel of career development and marriage, it has been twenty years since her last visit to Mungabareena. She avoids looking at the grey plastic box on the seat beside her – her heart would break if she did – and drives on. She turns down a rugged track beneath the cathedral arch of river-gum and across the cattle grid, so clogged with dirt the indolent cows inhabiting the reserve could wander freely – had the notion occurred.

This, her childhood playground, this sacred place, squats between the durable Murray River and the tree-covered range of the Eastern Hills, and as the woman navigates pot-holes and a basking blue-tongue, joyous childish laughter springs from the past and she sees again, Uncle Freddy, eyes glittering merrily, offering the little girl a steer of the car.

The woman drives unconsciously, easily selecting the trail that leads to the river's edge. Stopping the car on a grassy knoll, she steps out and climbs down to a natural little beach, offering harbour from the swiftly flowing Murray. She stands with the cool, silky water rippling over her bare feet.

She closes her eyes.

A cockatoo cries brightly overhead and cicadas sing their summer song. Breathing deeply, she tastes the dry grass, the parched earth, and all millennia in this timeless Aboriginal land.

A shift in time and Uncle Freddy is beside her, nodding sagely. "*Ja, ist sehr schön*," he says. He is bare-chested, his skin the colour of beer, and the tattoo on his arm, souvenir of his 1931 national service with the Swiss army, is a faded blue.

"*Ja*," the woman repeats softly to herself. Opening her eyes, she stares, mesmerized, into the water's irregular patterns. The sun sparkling on its surface, dances like the grey-green eyes that shone with pride when the child overcame her fear and swam her first strokes in this pristine place.

But there is the tree she must find. One whose sturdy trunk out-spanned the child's thin arms, and whose branches hung low over the water – the one with the initials W B carved into its bark.

The woman returns to her car and reaches through the passenger window to retrieve the silent plastic box. It is less heavy than expected and has WILFRED BAUM typed on a label, stuck to its face.

"*Baum* means tree," Uncle Freddy told the child, and as they walked, two pairs of rubber thongs slapped against heels, and they lifted their knees high in the tall grass. The child squealed in delight when a grasshopper landed on her arm and the man paused to study the little creature's brown markings before it leapt away with a thrust from powerful hind legs. The leaves on the tall poplars, planted by the first Riverina pioneers, fluttered like applause on the breeze – for this beautiful, precious land had been here forever …

The woman traces the steps of the child and the man, and her heart turns over as she sees the brick toilet block, the electric barbeque, and a metal bin chained to a post, a collection of plastic bags and scraps at its base – stark and alien.

Weaving along the river's edge, she worries that time may have worn away the initials and makes an examination of each likely trunk, though so many majestic gums, ancient before she was born, now lay lifeless in the water, the earth eroded from their desperate grasp.

And then, she sees it; a silent sentinel, tall and strong, the scar in its bark just visible.

"Remember vhere to find zis tree," the man said to the child in the heavy accent that ostracised him when war came. Shunned and mistrusted in the city, he was accepted here – where the residents had time to understand that he was Swiss, not German. He became Freddy, took a job, adopted the district's footy team, and the locals laughed when he yodelled the theme song.

He loved the town folk with their true-blue country values, the bush animals, and the land. And he taught the child to breathe the eucalypts, to close her eyes and taste the rain, and to cherish the perfection of wild creatures, all too easily overlooked by those born to them.

This would be his eternal home, this place, where the woman now crouches, dashing tears from her eyes, and prising the small round seal from the top of the box.

The ashes are powdery, pale, and light as air. They form a hillock at the base of the tree where the river laps at their edge. She lingers, watching them dampen and melt into the ground where they become part of the earth, the tree, and the water.

And then she turns away, making a slow walk back to her car, the veil of time floating briefly aside as a child's sibilant voice asks, "Did you bring any toffees, Uncle Freddy?"

"*Ja*, but mind you eat your dinner vhen ve get home."

The woman climbs into the car and turns the key in the ignition. The cows raise heavy heads as she drives past, crosses the cattle-grid, and takes the road to the highway. Turning her face away from the relentless creep of project home and estate, she relegates her childhood to a special corner of her mind – these diamond-bright memories, to be preserved and handled with care.

And she thanks her god that Uncle Freddy will never know this progress, for he will walk forever among the river-gums and yodel with the kookaburras.

The brink

"I've been watching you." The man's voice echoed beneath the buzzing in her head as she stood on the railway platform. "I've been watching you, and I know what you're up to."

She waited quietly as a sleepwalker, ensnared in a vortex of blurred colour, light, and sound. A nightmare from which there was no waking; an ever faster spinning and whirring and downward spiraling.

Blinkered early morning commuters jostled one another beneath the scratchy recorded message announcing the approaching train was not stopping at this station – *Express train to Richmond, stand clear please, stand clear.*

She was calm, as calm as she'd ever been, and aware in some distant corner of her soul that it would be so easy, so very, very effortless, and yet, so liberating.

"Hey! I'm talking to you!"

With detachment, she realised the stranger must be addressing her, but the swirling eddy was clawing her down into its bottomless depths, deeper and deeper until all air was sucked out and all movement was weighted.

She was a spectator beyond the fishbowl and it wasn't happening to her – it never did. She could step aside at any time and let it happen to someone else. The blackened eyes, broken bones, and split lip – all of it – the irresistible imposition of a greater strength upon some other woman. It was that woman, the one who happened to look like her, who bore the shame, and the cloying fear, not the woman who stood now, with her mind silent and her heart dead.

He sounded as though he was beneath the sea, and she was vaguely aware that the stranger was attempting to penetrate her senses, "Hey! Hey miss!" She felt his eyes searching her face for some sign that he had pierced her shell.

It was the urgency of his tone that finally spiked some awareness into her vacant stare. His compelling voice separated itself from the cacophony of crowd and clanking machinery and forced her eyes to focus. Robotically, her head turned to where he stood beside her.

"I know what you're gonna do," he said plainly, "and I'm not gonna let you. Why don'tcha take a step back?"

From somewhere else, she looked down. Her feet seemed small and unfamiliar, and such a long way away, teetering at the very edge of the platform. She swayed slightly and heard his quick intake of air.

"Hey listen," he said carefully. "I dunno what's going on, y'know. I ... I dunno what you're dealing with here ... but if you gotta ... like ... do it ... well, not in front of all these people. Not like this." His voice was low and gentle, reaching her at some long-forgotten level and she looked at him, seeing him for the first time.

He was young, perhaps early twenties – no older than herself – and dressed in a conservative navy business suit. A rolled up newspaper was in one hand, the other hovered uncertainly in her direction. His eyes were intense pebbles, his jaw was set hard, and she could see the fear he was trying to hide.

"Don't do it to him," he continued, nodding to the train that was hurtling toward the platform. "The driver ... he doesn't deserve it."

Everything around her was moving in slow-motion – the passage of time having no meaning. Trance-like, she dragged her head to the right as the train drew closer. The man at the controls, wide-eyed with horror, waved one arm in a frantic under-water gesture while the other leaned on the horn.

She watched impassively as the train neared and the driver's face contorted desperately in an inaudible scream of warning.

Every event of every day of her life had been a step on the path to this juncture. Every poor decision, every disappointment, each and every loss and unforgivable failure, all culminated here and now, at this crystallisation of time and space. How she longed for blessed oblivion. To escape the fear lurking at the house that wasn't a home; the menacing, soul-destroying, violent one who came under the guise of love.

The oncoming train pushed the air before it and dust blew about her face.

Capitulation came easy, then her body moved forward of its own accord.

In an explosion of movement he was upon her, grasping her around the arm, bruising her viciously, throwing her backwards so that for a second of frozen time her foot hung in mid-air.

He made no allowance for gentleness – she landed hard. Awaking as one from a shocking dream, she stared at the stranger leaning over her. His face was red and perspiring, and his eyes were grey, hard, and uncompromising. "Not here," he said firmly and shook his head, "not today."

The pedestrian tide parted, unmoved and insensible around them, barely noticing as he helped her to her feet. As the train crashed past, his newspaper, forgotten on the ground, unfurled and scattered along the platform. Her hair, blasted by the train's slipstream, pasted itself to the tears on her cheeks.

The glove

I'd heard the talk – whispers behind silk fans, and I'd seen the smirks, deliberately inadequately hidden. Even as I moved through the crowd of well-wishers, the tall man with good-looks enough for two at my side, I could not allow myself even a small fancy, for the society cats with their false smiles and claws sprung for the kill, hissed of the money I was to inherit.

My betrothal to John Falconer, impoverished lord with a title for auction, had been announced amid much fanfare. Painfully aware that he did not return my affection, my unfortunate face required I rely on my more fiscal attributes – and these he found irresistible.

On the morning of our engagement party he arrived, handsome, and citrus and clove scented, and presented with a flourish, a beautifully boxed betrothal gift.

I wanted to rush him, grasp him in a passion of love and happiness, but inherent shyness forestalled me. Sitting incongruously with my ill-favoured face above my pretty dress, I balanced the box on my knee and slipped its satin bow. Absorbed in my pleasure, I was unprepared for the explosion. His palm slammed the table and he barked, "Good grief Margaret! We are to be wed – can you not show the *slightest* emotion?"

I stared, wide-eyed and shocked. "John … I –"

In two strides he was dragging me to my feet, the box falling unnoticed to the rug as he kissed my mouth hard.

There was no love in it – only frustration, then he flung himself away to stare at the textured palm-frond wallpaper.

I touched my lips longingly, and stared at his back knowing that there were others whose wealth could as easily buy his fine name. But I loved him – desperately – and brimming with unaccustomed daring, I moved toward him.

In that exact moment he turned. "Margaret my dear, forgive me … I behaved terribly." His eyes were pleading and insincere – how desperate his need for my money – and my fleeting release from inhibition was lost. "Open your gift – please."

The opened box exuded a strong animal aroma, then the softest pair of white, kid gloves in creation. I adored them, kept touching them reverently, and couldn't wait to wear them, to silence forever those slanderous muck-rakers. And when we stepped out together, my hand on his arm, all of London would know his commitment to me.

We ate small cakes and drank chocolate, and he inquired like a polite acquaintance after the wedding plans, and later, after he was gone, I held the gloves against my cheek, breathing their velvety coolness.

———

I wore them for the first time the day Mamma and I went shopping for the wedding, and under Papa's instruction to *spare no expense*, Mamma complied with spirited obedience.

London in the summer; crowded, dirty and suffocating, was assaulting our senses, and Mamma suggested a refreshing glass of lemonade. We stepped inside the Silver Spoon Café and ordered our drinks. Mamma deigned to buy a small cup for the lad carrying our boxes. He gulped it cheerfully on the stoop, and I envied the unconscious freedom that comes with no appearances to be kept and no-one to comment, as he wiped his mouth on his sleeve.

I smiled, imagining Mamma's outraged expression if I should do likewise, and then I saw him and my smile froze. His beautiful face turned attentively to the handsome blonde on his arm. She was cool and shimmering in mint silk while the diamonds bobbing in her ears caught the sun jauntily as her head moved in animated conversation.

They paused, framed by the door as though for me alone. With her silken hand against his cheek, he turned his head and kissed her palm. A casual observer could not doubt their love. My pain was white and mind-numbing. I forced air into my lungs while every cell within me screamed in grief.

They moved on and I sat very still, my thoughts in turmoil. He had never, ever, looked at me with any sign of affection, yet here he was in London's full view …

The weeks passed and as the cats began to yowl the louder, I learned her name was Isabelle. I endured the talk with a practiced calm; witty, attractive, stylish, she merely lowers her lashes and the men come running; one man in particular. They said he'd been *seen* with her, *frequently*.

Mamma was dismissive. "It's of no consequence. You will marry, and once the marriage tree bears fruit, he may philander where he will – it's a man's way, you know."

Lure him to the altar on the strength of my inheritance? Gain myself a title? Little I cared for a title – I wanted his love.

"Continue planning the wedding and be seen with him often," was Mamma's sage advice.

And so I did. I wore my gloves proudly throughout that autumn, and my love grew with every day. I envisioned his blossoming love of me, his pride in our children, and the gloves kept a place of honour on my dresser beside the miniature of my handsome fiancé, my John.

Then one afternoon, Mother's friend, Adelaide, burst into our parlor like a pink whirlwind. Her flaccid cheeks were trembling, her hair awry, and she clasped my hands urgently.

"Isabelle has gone to Venice," she gasped. Mamma ordered tea and bade her friend becalm herself.

The talk in recent months had increased though I'd remained bland of face and square of shoulder throughout, and whilst John's attentiveness to me could not be faulted, I was weakening. Now, I sat breathing carefully while the conversation washed back and forth.

"My brother-in-law – ship owner, you know – was at the docks yesterday." Adelaide went on to describe a most attractive lady of obvious means, boarding a passenger liner bound for Italy. "Curiosity led to discreet enquiry. Turns out, the lady was none other than Isabelle Di Costa, returning to her – *you'll never believe* – estranged and *very* wealthy husband in Venice."

Adelaide sat back and arranged her face into a look of satisfaction but Mamma demurred, assuring her guest that it was quite irrelevant to us.

So I knew now why he would marry me over her – while both wealthy, I happened to be unencumbered.

———

The wedding preparations continued through the winter and the time of my spring nuptials drew closer. Fortunately Mamma took charge, leaving me free to be with my betrothed.

He visited regularly and dutifully, escorting me to the theatre, to balls and dinners. We rode through the snow in Hyde Park and dined in restaurants, and always, I wore the gloves.

Sadly, he made no further attempt to kiss me, though one afternoon, bundled against the cold in his carriage, I felt uncommonly bold. Reaching, ostensibly to point something out, I let my curls brush his cheek. He appeared surprised but not unhappy with my familiarity, whilst I reveled in newfound confidence. Moving ever so slightly, he rested his leg against mine, and held my hand for the remainder of our journey. I was, nevertheless, intensely aware that I competed with one whose power had not been diminished by absence.

A week before my wedding, Mamma and I were returning from an evening visit when she turned to me, her voice scoring the night with painful truth. "Honestly Margaret, you've the vivacity of a newel. You must have confidence in yourself to … captivate him – take his mind from her."

We entered the house and a maid removed our hats and coats. Mamma stood by the hall table watching me in the mirror as she stripped the evening gloves from her hands. "You'll be forever fighting if you – oh, there's a letter for you."

The envelope sat on a little silver message tray and I eyed it with foreboding as Mamma continued, "Think on my words … wed him and get yourself with child before you lose him to that woman." She swept up the stairs and her door banged shut, echoing in the quiet house.

In the privacy of my room, I read the note with a thudding heart and wanted to cry out to Mamma that it was too late.

The following morning in compliance with the message's instructions, I entered the Silver Spoon Café at the appointed time. The table was reserved in his name and I was shown to it. He arrived not two minutes later, pausing briefly on the threshold to look around. The familiar surge of love and pain mixed near choked me.

Taking his seat, he offered a distracted greeting and ordered coffee for himself and black tea for me. He sat fidgeting vaguely with his cravat and I wanted to scream, but of course, I sat quietly with eyes downcast so I couldn't see his lies as he told me of a sick friend.

Our marriage was to be delayed. "Not cancelled, of course," he added quickly, "and only until I return to England."

He couldn't be sure when that would be, but knew I'd understand, I was after-all, such a kind, caring girl.

"I shall be sailing to France in the morning, then boarding a train to Italy – cheaper, you see."

Italy? Why of course, that's where his … er … *friend* lived. And he went on …

… And I studied my hands, placed demurely in my lap. Each encased in its white kid glove. I stared long and hard at the soft leather, tight-fitting gloves reaching halfway to my elbow. I saw the miniscule pores in the skin, and felt the flex allowed my fingers. I could touch his cheek now and he would wonder at my soft caress.

My focus never strayed as I took in each unique natural mark in the hide lest my concentration falter, and my ears hear, and my heart cease its beating. I examined each fold, line and crease – I'd never noticed them before …

He was going to her and I would steel myself and not show my grief, *I must not show my grief*. If he would go to her, he would take something of me, and I would retain the other – each useless without its partner – like a name without a fortune …

His handsome face was taut. He sensed my resolve, and watched as I lifted my left hand; a gentle tug on the smallest finger, feeling the loosening and the resistance. Then, the next finger – the little bulge of diamond beneath – the middle finger, and the last – one by one, all loosened.

Withdrawing my hand, the glove came free in a rush, irreversible and final.

The whiff of animal caught briefly in my nostrils, I blinked once quickly, and folded it fingers under, and placed it beside the tea pot.

Our eyes met. There was much to say but no words adequate. I wanted to beg, or promise, or threaten, or tell him how much I loved him for, *God help me*, I did!

He did not love me, but perhaps in that moment he might admire me, for he understood what I knew, and he was not an unfeeling man, merely one who had fallen where his head had not directed.

Yet, he would leave my wealth, and destroy his good name for no society mamma would receive him again. I did not hope she proved worth the price – I was incapable of such magnanimity.

So be it. I would bear the shame of rejection; tell of the sick friend, outwardly preserving both our dignities – as if we fooled anyone!

As he rose to leave, I pushed the glove toward him – this glove, this gift, this insincere promise. For what use one glove? In time, he would come to learn his mistake for however humiliating, however painful, I would accept no reconciliation.

I said, without hesitation though my voice was a thin whisper, "Take this then, and carry it with you always. Let it ever remind you of your loss."

The silver lining

Rain dribbled sullenly down the glass. Little capillaries, that trickled and joined to form rivulets, meeting, gaining momentum, on their way to the window-sill.

Tammy adjusted her focus and gazed longingly at the chair in the garden. It was old, with peeling paint and positioned to catch the afternoon sun. Grumpily she let out her breath and cocked her head to look up at the sky. There would be no sun this afternoon and her chair was sodden.

It was cosy inside, but she was making a little fog patch on the glass, and though she was warm, she gave a little shiver, fluffing up her fur. Beyond the comfort of the living room, it was grey and wet, and sleeping in the sun on her favourite seat was unlikely today. She flicked her tail petulantly.

A sleepy sigh from the couch across the room distracted her and Tammy turned her fine head toward its source. Her eyes narrowed contemptuously as she studied him. Bones was fat, orange, and complacent. Subsisting only to eat and sleep on his favourite fluffy rug, he was younger than she, but lazy and indulged.

Tammy drew herself up and tucked her tail around her hind legs. Smooth-coated, sleek and striped, she groomed in private, and moved deliberately. *She* did not leave little clumps of fur on the carpets.

She was independant and reserved and preferred her own company, and though her intelligent eyes often followed the humans, she lacked the confidence to share her space with them.

Bones had an easy way with them, and they lavished their attention over him in return as he arched his curving back against their hands, and curled his tail around their legs. He was never shy of jumping onto a stranger's lap to solicit pats and praise.

Adversely, when strangers came to the house, Tammy would hide. Once, when a visitor came, Tammy had mustered all her boldness and approached timidly. The visitor, not noticing her sitting shyly by his foot, had suddenly moved and kicked her. Tammy's almost apologetic yowl of surprise caused him to drop a cup of something hot on the rug, leaving a stain and breaking the cup. She glanced at the brown mark now, her sensitive nostrils twitching as they picked up a whiff of its pungent smell, forever embedded in the carpet to remind her of her folly.

No – she was much better off on her chair outside in the sun; if only the black clouds would drift away.

Bones opened his green eyes slightly and yawned. Stretching his front legs before him, he gripped his rug in his claws and began to knead it, making kittenish, sucking sounds with his lips. His eye-lids drooped dreamily as he performed his little ritual, carefully giving no outward sign that he knew Tammy was watching. A low rumble vibrated rhythmically in his throat – indeed, life was truly good. Contentedly, his eyes closed, his movements became sluggish, his head dipped, and he slept again.

Tammy returned to her study of the garden as Tess bounded into view. Leggy and blonde, the lumbering dog grinned amicably as she cantered across the lawn toward her food bowl. She made a quick inspection – nothing had found its way there, no matter – her tail lifted happily and she trotted off, going about her business, unhampered by the ill-weather.

Rethinking the situation Tammy stood, stretched her serpentine body, and stepped gracefully into thin air, landing soundlessly on the carpet, before warily making her way to the porch door.

She did not yowl like Bones did when he wanted something. Tammy did not mew or plead with her snake eyes. Instead, she sat quietly and waited. At her position by the door, someone would pass by and see her sitting patiently.

It wasn't long before the voice of the she-human said, "You wanna go out?"

Tammy blinked.

"You won't like it out there today," the woman continued, but Tammy stood and pointed her face to the door. "Okay, but don't say you weren't warned."

The door slid open a crack and a blast of icy air hit Tammy in the face, but she was committed now, and challenged the elements bravely. This was her domain, and despite the first smack from the cold wind, she stepped lightly outside.

The sound of the door clicking shut notified the dog, and Tess, all tongue and slobber and eyes alert for a game, galloped toward her. Tammy turned her small body away from the dog who stood three times as tall as she, and feigning disregard, stepped delicately onto the lawn, charting a course for her seat.

Tess, oblivious to the obvious, performed the play-bow and danced around hopefully.

Arriving at her destination, Tammy leapt smoothly onto the chair, whiskers twitching in distaste as the rain-warped wood oozed water beneath her paws.

Tess advanced, eying Tammy nose to nose and Tammy, emboldened and harried, raised a warning paw. Tess had seen this before and knew the drill. Discouraged, she withdrew, her barometric tail limp before springing upright as she remembered the plant she'd been enthusiastically digging out when she'd been disturbed. She disappeared around the corner to complete her task.

The wind blew again and Tammy directed an accusing glare at the trees bending their backs and flapping their leaves threateningly toward her. Her fur rippled, and she hunched miserably into herself as the wind, icy and damp, grew stronger.

Suddenly, a deafening growl came from the animal in the sky. Tammy had heard this animal before but never when she was outside. Her eyes widened as the rumble of the animal's growl vibrated through her little body. Tess, with dirt on her nose, shot across the yard and threw herself into her kennel while Tammy stubbornly braced herself, ready to flee but careful not to show her fear lest the animal in the sky saw her. If the animal attacked she would defend herself, and, she supposed ruefully, that spineless, bungling mutt as well, who even now was cowering in her kennel.

With darting eyes and straining ears, she anticipated the animal's approach. The growl came again – louder this time. It was right above her head! Frozen with dread, her great yellow eyes were scanning the chunky black clouds when they opened up.

Water fell like it had been poured from a bucket, right over the top of her. Tammy screamed with rage and shock mixed. Her muscles jerked into action, all self-respect gone, as she leapt from her chair like a saturated mop. In three bounds she was back at the door, where she crouched trembling.

Tammy pressed her drenched body to the glass door leaving fur patterns on it, and she wailed frantically as a puddle formed around her.

And still the animal growled. The wind snapped a branch from a tree and threw it at her. Tammy screamed again and hammered her delicate paws on the door.

Though her voice was drowned in the din, she continued her bawling, all the while her fastidiously groomed stripes ran into each other and her normally pert tail dragged like a bloated slug behind her.

The wind persisted and the animal growled, and Tammy, pawing in terror at the door, yowled at the full pitch of her lungs. Suddenly, a brilliant flash cracked open the sky and Tammy, terrorised into silence, cringed into the door-frame.

Since there was no response from the she-human, Tammy dared a glance over her shoulder and hesitated. Tess' kennel was large, cosy and dry. The dog was huddled inside on a thick rug, and there was room for one more – particularly one as small as Tammy. As the idea grew in Tammy's mind, Tess stared through the bars of the rain and closed her expression – there is no invitation here; there is no welcome.

The animal continued to growl, each shuddering rumble growing louder, and the sky flashed bright and brittle setting Tammy's whiskers aquiver with static. The creature was directly above her preparing to pounce. She could imagine him hunkered low, back-end coiled in readiness. He was so close he could swallow her and yet she couldn't see him!

Horror made her panic. Sucking in a chest full of air, she turned back to the door but her cry caught in her throat. On the other side of the glass sat Bones; secure, self-satisfied and smug. Licking his chops like he'd just eaten a succulent slice of chicken, he turned slowly from the door and sidled away, tail high and triumphant.

There is no dignity in such distress, and Tammy wailed pitifully, her little voice breaking in anguish, her fine-boned body quaking with fear and cold.

Suddenly legs appeared – the she-human, she was there! The door slid back and Tammy was scooped into a plump, warm towel.

"Oh my goodness, you're soaked!" the woman said. "And you're freezing too. Let's get you to the heater, shall we?"

Tammy was carried in the towel to the room with the talking box. The she-human knelt on the rug before the heater and Tammy breathed in the familiar homely scents on the towel as it was fluffed over her wet body. Warmth began to penetrate her chilled skin and her trembling subsided, but her muscles remained warily alert, ready to spring at the slightest hint of … anything.

After much attention with the towel, the she-human finished her work but remained squatting on the floor, making no move to leave. Tammy's fear had worn her out, and having no desire to be alone, she allowed the she-human's gentle hands and soothing words to relax her taut muscles.

Finally, as the storm outside abated, Tammy's fur dried and her body's temperature righted itself. The woman stood up and said, "Alright now girl? I know you don't like cuddles, so I'll leave you be."

The legs moved away and Tammy stared after them, feeling uncommonly small and alone. Crossing the room, the she-human sat on the couch next to Bones' vacant fluffy rug, and sounds came from the talking box.

Tammy hovered undecidedly, wary of approaching, yet not ready to relinquish the comfort she'd experienced in the she-human's arms. She cast a furtive peek into the next room. Bones was nowhere in sight – it was worth a try.

Mindful that Bones could re-appear at any second, she cautiously made her way across the room until she was at the she-human's knee.

"Hello girl. Had enough of the heater?"

Tammy risked a glance upward and met soft brown eyes and a welcoming smile. The she-human smoothed her skirt across her lap.

After only a moment's hesitation, Tammy sprang lightly onto the she-human's legs. Unaccustomed to the feeling, she paused unsteadily for a moment, but with the she-human's gentle strokes and soft feminine voice, she finally let her overwrought body unwind.

"Now this *is* unusual behaviour from you," the woman said. "You must've had a nasty scare out there today."

Bones chose that moment to come into the room. His assured stride faltered at the sight of Tammy on the she-human's lap and though his eyes narrowed, his pause was only momentary. Recovering quickly, he barely missed a beat as he changed direction. Stopping before the heater, he sat and stared intently across the room.

Since the she-human made no move to banish her, Tammy settled with new confidence, but kept her eyes and ears alert. The she-human's warmth was seeping into her and it quietened her. An uncertain purr sounded in her throat and grew stronger as the tension ebbed away.

In time, Tammy's eyes began to droop and her head nodded. Her throat vibrated and sent pleasant little rumblings through her ribs and down along her spine. Abandoning all caution, she curled herself into a donut shape and tucked her tail beneath her chin.

Tammy's eyes closed contentedly.

The glass

The mirror, when Lizzie brought it home from the garage sale, was large, oval-shaped, and dirty-glassed. Its reflective backing was mottled with age and the ornate frame was grimy and colourless, but a rub with a licked finger revealed gleaming gold leaf. It had potential, and now, it had a new home.

It took Lizzie a month of weekends, painstakingly, with warm soapy water and a soft-bristled brush, to extract years of muck from the intricate creases and folds of the frame. Vinegar, and a measure of elbow grease, had the glass as clean as it would ever be.

Lizzie watched her brother drill a hole and insert the hook. Ben grunted as he lifted the heavy ornament into place. Standing back, hands on hips, he considered the effect.

Lizzie wanted it hung in the hall, which didn't enjoy any natural light, so it could reflect the glow from the sconce on the opposite wall. Her mouth curved up with satisfaction at the result.

"Thanks bro."

"You like it?" he asked, doubtfully.

"Yep. Don't you?"

He shook his head. "It's too big and old."

"This is an old house," said Lizzie, cheerfully.

He shrugged. "Your house, your choice. Gotta go, seeya at Mum's on Sunday."

Closing the door behind him, Lizzie turned back to the mirror. It reminded her of something she couldn't place, but it was a comfortable feeling nonetheless.

Sunday roast at her mother's had been tradition since Lizzie's father had died last year, and nothing short of serious illness was considered an acceptable excuse for absence. That Sunday, Lizzie checked her look in her new mirror before leaving the house. The mirror was large enough for her to see herself from the waist up. She wore peach lip-gloss and a touch of brown mascara – her only concessions to make-up; her smooth, thirty-something complexion needed no garnish.

She had on a striped shirt with the top two buttons undone – nice, but … something didn't sit right.

Spinning on her heel, she ran to her room, gathered bobby-pins, hairbrush, and hairspray. Returning to the hall, she brushed her chestnut hair, coiled and pinned it with an unconscious deftness, into an elegant chignon. Carefully, she pulled out little strands beside her ears and wound them into curling tendrils to frame her face. A veil of spray, and she was done.

Pleased, she left the house.

"What's with the hair?" said Ben, as Lizzie took her seat opposite him.

Lizzie smiled happily. "Thought I'd try something new. Like it?"

He shook his head and spooned roasted vegetables onto his plate. "It's a bit daggy."

"I like it," their mother said, "it's nice – old fashioned, shows your cheekbones." Shirley patted Lizzie's cheek affectionately.

"Well, I like it too," Lizzie said.

"You have nice cheekbones," her mother continued. "You know, I was only saying to Maureen the other day, that young ones nowadays have their hair all over the place. And dirty! Good heavens, they're all afraid of soap. I said to Maureen, 'they never use soap these days, Maureen,' and she agreed. Her neighbour's daughter –"

"Okay Ma, we get the picture," Ben said rolling his eyes at Lizzie. "Chuck us the beans, will ya Liz."

Lizzie grinned across the table and passed her brother the bowl of green-beans, steaming and fragrant with butter and herbs.

***

Leaving her mother's later than usual, it was dark when Lizzie arrived home. She closed the front door behind her, and flipped the switch to illuminate the hall in warm, yellow light. The mirror opposite picked up the glow and threw the elaborate cornices and old plasterwork into shadowed relief.

The light wasn't very bright and she stood before the mirror, straining to see her reflection. Her mother was right; the hairstyle did suit her cheekbones. Lizzie yawned – time for bed.

She was about to walk away, when something caught her attention and she hesitated. Peering into the mirror, Lizzie thought the sconce on the wall was reflected oddly. Perhaps it was the effect of the light being echoed in the glass, or perhaps the aged glass itself, but ... she shook her head. *That can't be right.*

She looked over her shoulder at the wall-lamp. It was a polished brass bowl with a globe sitting upright within it. Nothing strange about that, but the mirror …

She turned back and squinted, a small crease forming between her brows. She could swear the reflected globe was slightly larger, with a little yellow flame dancing inside.

Such a strange trick of the light. She chuckled to herself and went to bed.

Lizzie worked for an accounting firm. Her new hairstyle that Monday morning occasioned more than a few second glances. Joan, the well-matured tea-lady, made a point of saying how nice it was.

"Reminds me o' me ol' mum," she said wistfully in her plummy accent.

Kylie-of-the-younger-set, stood before Lizzie's desk. "Did you go to a wedding yesterday, Liz?" she asked.

Uncertain what to make of that, Lizzie smiled politely, and wondered if she ought to introduce Kylie to Ben. Kylie sidled away and Lizzie went back to adding figures on her calculator.

During lunch, Lizzie went shopping. Her new hair-do warranted new clothes, and though she couldn't quite picture what she wanted, she'd know when she saw it.

Assorted garments, on endless racks and shelves at the large department store, offered up nothing suitable, and Lizzie's dismay grew as her lunch-hour dwindled. Irresolute, she stood outside on the street. She really should be getting back to work but there must be somewhere else she could quickly check.

Suddenly her eyes lit on a mannequin posed in a charity shop across the road. *That's it – perfect!*

Twenty minutes later, a large parcel under her arm, Lizzie arrived back at the office. She'd bought so much, the sales lady had thrown in a beautiful pair of dangly earrings for free. Lizzie couldn't wait to get home.

That evening, standing before the mirror, Lizzie examined her new outfit. Her hair was coiled into a knot on her crown, with cascades of curls tumbling over her shoulders. Faceted, red-glass earrings bobbed jauntily from her ears, and the fine cotton blouse, one of her charity-shop purchases, fitted perfectly. It had a high lace collar and a delicate lace panel down the front. She smiled at her reflection.

Lizzie was growing accustomed to the dimness of the flickering light reflected in the mirror – in fact she quite liked the moodiness of it. She also liked the way it gave the reflected wall behind her a textured appearance, almost like it was covered in some kind of old-style wallpaper.

The office girls were quite trendy and Lizzie felt certain they'd like her new look, so she began introducing some of her charity clothes to her work wardrobe. Over the next few days, she visited her new favourite shop again, and picked up a few more items – among them, a classy little marcasite brooch, that she wore pinned at the throat of her cream silk blouse.

By the weekend, she'd accumulated quite a collection. Standing before the mirror, she was very pleased with her new appearance. She popped a little straw bonnet onto her head and looped the ribbon beneath her chin. Stepping out into the Saturday afternoon sunshine, she opened her pretty, frilled parasol and took a turn around the neighbourhood.

"Holy cow! What's with the get-up?" Ben exclaimed as she walked into their mother's kitchen that following Sunday.

"Please restrain yourself, Benjamin," Lizzie admonished, taking her seat at the table.

"*What?*" said her brother, his eyes widening in surprise.

"I think she looks lovely," Shirley said, smiling indulgently at her daughter.

"Hmph, you're both nuts," Ben said. He took a companionable beer from the fridge.

"It's just a phase she's going through," their mother went on, "like the velvet pedal-pushers. Begged me to buy them, had to have them or she'd die. Well, she got them all right, and the very next year, they weren't in fashion anymore – never saw the light of day again. This'll be the same, a phase, mark my words. I was only saying to Maureen the other day …"

"Dumb phase," Ben muttered. He tuned out and watched the bubbles in his beer rise to the surface of his glass and form a half-inch, creamy foam at the top.

That evening, Ben offered to drive Lizzie home. Pulling up the driveway, he watched his sister climb out of the car and his lips pursed thoughtfully. "What's going on Liz?" the wave of his hand indicated her hair and clothes. "It looks really silly. If it's some kind of joke …"

Lizzie stared at him. "I don't understand you. I look nice – even Mum said so."

"It's silly," her brother said again.

"Oh, you've never had any fashion sense," she said flatly and turned indignantly. Her long skirt whispered silkily as she strode up the path to her door.

Closing the front door, she flipped on the light and stripped off her long kid gloves. She folded them neatly, before absently letting them drop to the floor. Ben was certainly acting strangely – even for him.

Standing before the mirror, her assessment confirmed Lizzie had never looked so fine; elegantly dressed hair, stylish clothes, tasteful jewellery. She stood for some minutes, and her hazel gaze drifted away from her own image, to the sconce on the wall behind her, with the little flame flickering away. It illuminated the muted colours of the striped wallpaper, the wrought-iron hat-rack where her bonnets hung with their trailing ribbons and silk flowers, and the hall-stand with its heavy wooden legs and carved ivy twining its way up the intricate frame. Her gloves were folded neatly on its polished surface and her parasols sat in the umbrella stand, their handles poking out of the purpose-cut hole, beside the silver calling-card tray.

Monday arrived and Lizzie was feeling good about herself.

"Are you in some sort of play or something?" Kylie asked. Lizzie raised her eyes from her work. The young girl was slouching casually before Lizzie's desk, her slacks were slung low on her hips, and her closely fitted polyester top was exposing an unseemly amount of flesh above her belt.

Lizzie's response was tight with disapproval, "No, why?"

Kylie shrugged. "Just wondering. You kinda look like you're in an old costume. It's weird that's all … " her voice trailed off uncertainly. Lizzie watched the girl leave and decided a match with Ben would be most inappropriate after all.

With some annoyance, Lizzie returned to her notepad – she'd have to start totalling the figures all over. She took up her pencil, and began again …

That evening, when she arrived home, Ben was waiting on the porch for her.

"Good afternoon," she said cheerfully as she strolled up the driveway.

His eyes sifted over her and he frowned. "Hi."

Following her inside, he gazed around, blinking in bewilderment. "Will you be staying for dinner?" she asked politely.

Ben turned to his sister. "Liz, what's going on?"

"Whatever do you mean?" Lizzie said, untying her bonnet and moving as though to hang it, but letting it fall carelessly to the floor.

"What are you doing?" her brother said, staring at the pile of hats, shawls, parasols and various other items on the floor. "What's all this stuff doing here? And you – you're talking funny."

"I'm sure I don't understand you, Benjamin. Hang up your hat and let's get you a lemonade."

Ben involuntarily touched his bare head in confusion. "No … stop! Liz, look at this stuff. What *is* all this?"

"Oh," she waved her hand breezily, "I've been shopping lately that's all – you wouldn't understand."

"You got that right," he said, "so how about explaining."

"Never mind." She went to move away but he gripped her elbow and held her.

"I want to know, and I'll try to understand, I promise. Try me." His voice was gentle and his eyes, normally so blue, were cloudy with concern. She hesitated.

"I'm a woman, Benjamin, I can't wear the same clothes everyday."

"You wear these *out*? To *work*?" He took her hands, "Liz –"

"What's got into you?" she asked. Pulling away from him, she scrutinised her reflection, patted her hair and smoothed her long woollen skirt. The potted palm in the corner looked a bit wilted, "I keep forgetting to water that," she said pensively.

"What?" he said at her shoulder.

"The plant," she said nodding to its reflection, "needs water. I keep forgetting."

"What plant?" unease crept into his voice.

Sighing with exasperation, she said, "*That* plant," and stabbed a finger at the mirror, touching it lightly. With a sudden yelp, she leapt back in alarm and watched the spreading, liquid ripples run across the glass.

Ben was speaking but she was transfixed. The ripples disappeared as they neared the gilt frame. Cautiously, she stepped forward, hand raised, finger extended, and touched it again.

She gasped at the effect as once again little waves spread out, widened and faded.

She turned to him. "Did you see that?"

"See what?"

"The glass, it … it had ripples in it."

"It's old glass, it's probably not perfectly smooth."

"Not like that," she cried. "It moved when I touched it, like when you dip your finger into a pond."

He stared at her for a moment, and suppressed an untimely desire to laugh, then, moving her aside, he stepped closer to look into the mirror. There was no pot-plant, only a pile of Liz's bits and pieces haphazardly strewn about the floor, including the bonnet she'd been wearing when she came in. He touched the glass – it was cool beneath his fingers but certainly not liquid.

"Liz –"

"Did you see?" she asked eagerly. "You did, didn't you?"

The look on his face gave her the answer. She shouldered him out of the way. "Look!" Touching the mirror again, she held out her hand for his examination, "It's wet."

He didn't even give it a cursory glance. "Liz," he said, carefully choosing his words, "tell me what you see when you look in that mirror."

"Benjamin!"

"Just … just humour me, please?"

"You're being ridiculous," Lizzie said irritably. "I asked you to touch it."

"And I did, and I can see nothing unusual with it. But you reckon it moves and you can see a plant – there's *no plant* in this room."

Ben reached out to touch his sister gently, but she slapped his hand away. "I don't know what's wrong with you," she said. She turned back to the mirror and pointed. "Look, there's a pot-plant, a hall-stand, hat-rack – complete with my bonnets I might add – don't look like that, and don't tell me you can't see them!"

Ben sighed wearily. "I can't, and I think you're imagining these things."

Lizzie made an indelicate snorting noise, "You're intoxicated."

"Look around you!" he shouted, suddenly losing patience. Startled, Lizzie stared at her brother. His face had grown dark with anger and something else that looked a little like fear. She gasped as he gripped her chin. "Look Liz!" he demanded. "There's nothing here but a pile of old stuff – *look*!"

"No!" she squeaked, stubbornly squeezing her eyes closed.

"Liz, it doesn't make sense," he cried, mounting panic was making him cruel.

"You're hurting me," she whimpered.

"Fine!" Abruptly, he flung himself away and burst out the door into the declining daylight, to his car.

"Where are you going?" Lizzie called after him. She was rubbing her jaw as Ben pushed past her on his way back inside. He was clenching a large hammer tightly by its handle like he wanted to throttle it.

"What are you doing?" his sister cried with fright.

He didn't answer. He gripped the heavy thing in both hands and hauled it above his head.

Lizzie screamed, "*No!*" She grabbed his arm, hung off it, trying to stop him, and was successful for a moment, but then his strength won out.

"Get back!" he yelled and brought the hammer down with an almighty crash, sending glass shards in all directions.

Lizzie screamed again, and tears streamed down her face. "*No, Ben no … !*"

He paid her no attention as he wielded the hammer again, and again, breaking through the mirror's wooden backing and splintering the frame. Lizzie slumped to the floor amidst the devastation of shattered glass and wood.

Breathing heavily, his frenzy over, Ben's arms were aching with exertion by the time he dropped the hammer. It thumped with finality amongst the wreckage. Looking to his sister, he said gently, "Liz, are you alright?"

"My … mirror," she sobbed.

He shook his head. "There was something wrong with it, Liz. Look at yourself, look at your clothes."

As his words sunk in, she looked down at herself. The fine woollen skirt she was wearing, that had been so pretty and blue this morning, was faded and patched. Her crisp linen blouse was missing buttons and was frayed and wilted at the collar and cuffs.

"But … " she said, and her brow puckered in confusion. "I don't understand … "

"They were always like that," Ben explained carefully, "but that mirror … it was weird … somehow you couldn't see."

She shook her head and repeated, "I don't understand."

"Just look." He nudged a pile of old and threadbare clothes with the tip of his boot. Dust motes rose in the air and Lizzie caught the distinctively musty smell of aged fabric. "Look at all this stuff – this old garbage."

He helped her up, and watched her look around, following her slow acceptance of the reality before her.

Lizzie's eyes did a sweep of the room; no hall-stand, hat-rack, or potted palm, just a dim, high-ceilinged hallway with a massive pile of smelly old stuff on the floor. Finally, she turned to Ben, who was studying her closely.

"Liz?" he said uncertainly, "you okay?"

Self-consciously, she attempted a smile, and her breath came out in a rush. "Wow!"

On a churchyard wall

"But tha must sit there all neet," said the craggy old gent in a broad Yorkshire accent. "Takes patience and mickle courage but tha'll see … everyone does."

"You're talking about a ghost?" Zoe said in disbelief.

"Aye. A boggart."

Sipping her pint, Zoe glanced across at Cate. Travelling the English countryside together, the two girls had found themselves in quaint Little Gledhill where the buildings looked like doll-houses and time had bypassed the 175 residents. The weather-beaten farmer sat before them in an aged cable-knit jumper and flat-cap that looked like it had seen the Luddite Rebellion. With a pint of Theakston's Old Peculiar by his elbow, he was regaling the two *furrin lassies* with wild local tales.

Zoe's skepticism showed in her frown. The old chap smiled mysteriously. "Nae-believer? Pass a nect on yon wall … tha'll be changin' thee meend."

"Doubt it," Zoe replied, "I don't believe in ghosts."

"Wha' about thee friend, then?"

Cate grimaced. "No way. You might be just having a lend, but I'm not taking that chance. I'll be safe and warm in bed tonight. Zo …?"

Zoe shook her head. "It's all rubbish. I've never seen a ghost … I only believe in stuff I can see."

"One neet on t'wall … tha'll believe areet," the old timer said with conviction.

"Not scared?" Cate asked, and Zoe recognised the challenge in her friend's glinting hazel eyes and grimaced.

"Nup, just don't fancy sitting on a churchyard wall all night for some urban legend."

The farmer stiffly heaved himself off his bar-stool. "Don't tha be so sure, lassie. Legends start wi' summat."

He shuffled away to join a group of friends, all wearing the flat-cap and jabbering in the largely unintelligible local dialect.

"You don't believe?" Cate asked.

Zoe stared at her archly. "And you do? They probably tell the same old tale to every tourist – gives 'em a few laughs."

Cate shrugged. "If you're not scared, what's stoppin' you?"

"I'm not spending thirty-five pounds on a room so I can sit on a wall all night waiting for some fictional spook."

"You would for fifty pounds."

"Is that a dare?" Zoe slanted a suspicious look at her friend.

Cate winked mischievously. "I wanna see if you've got the guts."

"It's not about guts … it's gonna be cold out tonight."

"Fifty quid and a thermos of soup."

"And a Mars bar?"

"Oooh you drive a hard bargain," Cate said with a laugh. "Done!"

"Ah would'na reckoned tha'd do 't", old Brucie said, handing the girls a quickly scrawled map of where Zoe was to sit. "Come an' see's in t'mornin'."

The churchyard wall bordered a cobbled lane separating the church from the back of a strip of shops. Zoe followed her yellow torch-beam the twenty prescribed yards up the lane to the where a street-lamp offered an apathetic circle of light. The village clock was striking ten as she dropped her bag to the cobbles and pulled out a polar-fleece rug, then, aimed her torch at the low, blue-stone wall. It was pockmarked with age and patchy with grey lichen, but wide enough to make a reasonable seat. Snapping the torch off to preserve its battery, she spread her rug over the wall and hauled herself into position.

In the vague light from the street-lamp she could just make out the weathered headstones leaning at odd angles like crooked teeth in a great gaping mouth. Her dangling legs hung a mere three feet from the nearest. Zoe shivered involuntarily and reached behind to pull her bag up beside her.

"Shoulda brought my i-Pod," she muttered out loud. "Can't believe I'm doing this." Only the autumn leaves replied, whispering as they fluttered among the headstones. The cold of the stone wall was already seeping through the polar-fleece rug beneath her bum, and she wondered if her grandma was right about that causing piles. With the overhang of the blanket pulled about her shoulders and crossed over in front, she tucked the ends beneath her arms, freeing her hands so she could ferret around in her bag for Cate's thermos of tomato soup.

Scaredy-cat Cate.

Zoe had teased Cate for her willingness to be suckered into the locals' tales but Cate, for all her foolish gullibility, was now tucked up in a nice warm bed, while Zoe felt the night-time mist falling on her hair like a damp spider-web.

"Let's see if bravado keeps you warm," Zoe said sardonically, and cupped her hands around the mug of soup. In time, the village clock struck eleven and the kind of fog one would expect in an out-of-the-way Yorkshire village swirled insidiously about her ankles, dampening her jeans and chilling her feet despite the thick socks and boots she wore.

"It's Brigadoon," she joked in her best Scottish accent. Somewhere in the distance, a dog barked, its lonely sound echoed in the brittle night air and Zoe gratefully remembered the *Reader's Digest* she'd thrown into her bag at the last minute.

———

The village had fallen silent as the last of the pub-goers drifted home to their beds. Zoe had been reading for some time and her torch, which had put in a valiant effort, now faded to a pin-point of orange before petering out altogether. The magazine had taken her mind off the chill of the night, but now, after midnight – the witching-hour, her traitorous mind whispered – she was becoming aware of how cold she was. Her feet were numb in her boots and – she stiffened.

A noise … a scuffling of leaves … close by. Zoe strained her ears.

It came again … something was moving about … on the ground … just to her right.

Please let it not be a rat, she prayed silently.

Cursing her dead torch, Zoe pulled her knees up beneath her chin while her ragged breath formed white plumes that hung for a heartbeat before melting into the swirling fog. She widened her eyes, vainly attempting to penetrate the dark and floating mist, and clutched the rug tightly as the scuffling continued, scratching randomly through the grass and ground debris, and growing closer.

Mustering all her courage, she snarled, *"Go away!"*

Her voice sounded nervous and fell flat in the fog. She hoped to hear the creature scuttling into the distance but there was silence.

"*Ssssss,*" she hissed.

Still silence, then, a tentative, questioning, "*Miaow … ?*"

Zoe let her breath out in a rush and her shoulders relaxed with relief. "Puss? Come 'ere, puss … "

There was another mew and then Zoe gasped in surprise as a fat grey cat sprang with feline agility to the wall beside her. Its eyes glowed emerald beneath the street-lamp and Zoe reached out automatically to stroke it. Immediately its joyous purr filled the emptiness of the night and Zoe, more grateful of company than she would admit, pulled it onto her lap.

The cat's body rumbled as she held it against her, fortified by its warmth and friendship. As the village clock chimed twice, the cat burrowed beneath a fold of the polar-fleece and at length, Zoe's head nodded sleepily.

Zoe slept, comforted and warmed by the cat curled against her. She didn't hear the clock striking three, nor was she aware of the little brown stoat that snuffled among the headstones in search of mice. She only returned to consciousness when the cat leapt from beneath their blanket with a startled cry and melted into the shadows like a grey streak of vapour.

Zoe rubbed the stiffness from her neck and wondered what time it was. Angling her wrist toward the ineffectual street-lamp, she was attempting to read the time when she heard the rhythmic tramp of boots coming up the lane toward her. The footfalls echoed through the night bouncing off the cobbles in the thick fog.

Now, Zoe was afraid for what sort of weirdo walks the streets at this hour? She hugged the blanket, still warm from the cat, to her chin. Hair bristled on the back of her neck and she could hear the blood pounding in her ears. Irresolute, she hovered between braving it out and fleeing. Only her reluctance to hide in the graveyard … in the fog … in the dark – with or without ghosts – kept her on the wall.

The footsteps were drawing closer. Zoe held her breath, staring into the gloom as the figure emerged from the shadows. It stopped at the edge of the light, lingering for only a moment before approaching.

By the time he stood before her, Zoe breathed again for this was no weirdo – it was a boy, about fifteen, with light brown hair and a cheerful face.

His grin crinkled the corners of his eyes and he touched the tip of his flat-cap in greeting. "Tha's not from round 'ere."

Zoe shook her head, too relieved to speak.

"Ah kin tell as theys got tha sittin on yon wall. Tha must be daft … in this cold … "

"It is pretty cold." Zoe was feeling foolish and gave an embarrassed little laugh.

"Waitin' fer boggarts? Seen owt?"

She glanced about reflexively, as if the fabled ghost awaited such a cue. "No. Not a sign."

"Aye," he nodded knowingly. "And tha tells 'em so. Tells 'em thee sees nowt but Meechael on 'his way t'work."

He made to walk on but she was reluctant to be alone. "Work?" she said, quickly. "Who works at this hour?"

"Bakers do, mum. Up yon way … Green's Bakery, corner by t'Queen's 'Ead pub." He pointed up the lane beyond the street-light. "Must go … theys'll get a benny on if ah be late." He offered a brief salute and continued on his way. Zoe raised her hand in reply, feeling very alone as he disappeared into the shifting mist.

Stiff with cold and from sitting too long in the one position, Zoe moved carefully. Dawn had gilded the bellies of low hanging clouds and lightened the eastern horizon, chasing out fog and lurking shades, and revealing a slick of rime over all.

"Enough's enough," she said, unfolding herself from her scrunched position. She shook out the polar-fleece blanket, watching the fine grey cat-hairs come free, and folding it, she tried not to think about Brucie and his cronies at the pub, congratulating themselves on suckering in yet another tourist – though in truth they weren't entirely to blame. She stuffed the blanket into her bag and acknowledged wryly that her own perverse stubbornness had brought her here in the first place.

Hunger was twisting her stomach as Zoe let herself into the hotel room. Cate sat up in her bed and yawned.

"Well?" she asked sleepily. "Any spooks?"

Zoe flopped onto her own bed. "Not one, and now I feel so stupid 'cause they would've known all along."

"Don't worry. We'll never see them again."

"Crap!" Zoe declared. "We're going back to that pub and I'm gonna tell those old buggers exactly what I think of 'em. Coulda caught pneumonia out there … "

———

Zoe and Cate, not tall girls, were nevertheless forced to duck their heads as they entered the centuries-old Wheatsheaf Inn. Low, rough-hewn beams scored the ceiling and the yellowed off-plumb walls evidenced decades of poor ventilation.

Zoe spotted him at the bar beside a friend. Marching over, she prodded Brucie in the shoulder.

The old boy turned, saw her, and raised a quizzical eyebrow. "Well, lass – 'ow's thee neet?"

"You need to ask?" Zoe replied smartly. "I sat there freezing my toes off for nothing – as you well know. Hope you had a good laugh."

Brucie shot a peculiar glance at his companion, who said to Zoe, "Tha seen nowt?"

She shook her head. "Nowt – I mean nothing."

"Nowt …" Brucie repeated, and the other man frowned.

"Ah, but tha seen Meechael, reet?" Brucie asked.

Zoe nodded, "And the cat."

"Don't know nowt 'bout a cat, but tha spake wi' Meechael, reet?" Brucie's friend said.

Again Zoe nodded.

"And Meechael says where 'e be goin'?" said Brucie.

"To work … the bakery near the Queen's Head."

"Ah …" the two men said in unison and returned to their pints.

Zoe and Cate exchanged surprised looks.

"Is that it, then?" Cate asked.

"Aye lassies. Tha says tha seen nowt but Meechael … then thass all there be." Brucie grinned at the girls.

"Oh *ha-de-ha* – real funny joke," Zoe snapped contemptuously.

Brucie offered a rueful shrug. "None forced tha on t'wall. Tell tha wha'. Tha goes up t'Green's bakery an' tha tell's 'em auld Brucie sends tha. Theys'll give tha a malt-loaf fer tha trouble."

"Come on, Zo." Cate took Zoe's arm. "Hope you got your jollies," she threw over her shoulder as the girls left in disgust.

———

"I s'pose they think they're really clever," Zoe grumbled as they stood in the midst of the bustling village market-day.

"What would you expect though – we're tourists ... easy targets."

Zoe sighed through her nose. She'd be pleased to leave Little Gledhill, whose silly joke continued to rankle. "So, what do we do now?"

"Look around the market? Heaps to see."

"Okay, but I'm over this place. Let's head north a day early – Scotland, I'm looking forward to seeing Loch Ness."

"Oh goody! No more local legends for us!" Cate said with a smirk.

"Ha-ha ... whatever. But after that I'm definitely going up to that bakery to get a freebie malt loaf. Coming ... ?"

For the next hour, they trawled the winding cobbled lanes of the market enjoying the colour and noise. They bought local fudge, and some oranges from Spain, and laughed at one another trying on flat-caps. They scanned rows of second-hand paperbacks and avoided the fishmonger whose stock stared at them from opaque eyes.

Eventually, the lanes widened into streets with stone, single-fronted houses, and as the clatter and din of the market faded behind them they found themselves standing beside a vacant lot. It was a T-junction and the Queen's Head Hotel stood at the top of it and there was a petrol station on the opposite corner.

Zoe said, "That Michael guy's bakery was supposed to be near here I can't see it and I don't think we've passed it."

"You're sure he said Queen's Head? I could do with that malt loaf – I'm hungry."

"Yep, but he said it was on a corner – and there's the Queen's ... Cate? What're you doing?"

Cate had drifted away and was standing in the empty paddock, her back to Zoe, and when she turned her face was devoid of colour.

"You look like you've seen a ghost," Zoe called playfully, but sobered quickly as she took in her friend's expression. "Cate ...?"

Cate made no reply. She was staring at something. Suddenly dropping to the ground, she began tearing aside a curtain of crawling ivy to reveal a three foot pyramid of stone bearing a time-worn inscription.

"Oh my god," she breathed as Zoe approached and stood at her shoulder. "Read this."

Drawing a deep breath, Zoe read aloud;

*This monument was erected
by the townsfolk of Little Gledhill
in memory of Jack Green,
Timothy Lumsden and Michael Tibbs,
who lost their lives in the 1929 fire
that destroyed Green's Bakery.*

May their ashes Rest In Peace.

Stranger on a train

The grey suit was inappropriate for her 19 years making her look frumpy and angular, but the 60 something manageress at the handbag shop, deemed it suitable for their customers, and the inexperienced girl knew no better.

It was late. A last minute, *just browsing thanks,* meant she'd missed her train, and now, waiting that extra hour to catch the next one was exhausting. Her feet ached cruelly in their black vinyl courts, and her ankles had swollen like her Grandma's did. Finally, she boarded the train.

There were girls in the carriage, of an age with her, made-up and dressed for a night out. Their budgie-chatter bounced around the carriage, but as she entered, there was pause, a comment, a giggle, then their conversation resumed.

She knew she looked dowdy, she also knew that her plain face and non-descript hair didn't help. She made her way to the vacant seat at the front of the carriage, the better to read her book in peace, rather than face the ones she envied. It wasn't their fault she felt thus, but neither was it hers. She simply lacked the confidence to be like them.

She slumped in her seat anticipating a long journey and pulled a glossy-fronted bodice-ripper from her bag. She opened it at the bookmark – a faded strip of embroidered fabric with a tatty, tasseled fringe – that had been her mother's and was now hers.

Her brothers always laughed at her choice of literature, but she read these books, living her life vicariously through the dangerous adventures of raven-haired beauties, or fiery red-headed vixen, loved by heroes and fueled by courage and passion.

The trained jolted convulsively stopping at the first of 26 stations, but engrossed in her book, Nell's first awareness of company was when the stranger sat down. The girl groaned and stretched her legs along the three empty seats opposite Nell.

Nell furtively took in the bleached hair and smudged black mascara before averting her eyes, and when the girl groaned again and shifted restlessly, Nell tensed. The stranger was probably *on* something and Nell prepared to change seats, or perhaps, run to another carriage at the next stop.

Suddenly, the stranger's hand flew to her hip and she gave a soft cry. Nell cautiously raised her head. The girl was wearing a black singlet-top and leather thong around her neck. A large, colourful tattoo – a dragon with twin plumes of flame from its distended nostrils – lapped at her neck, its tail slashed, sickle-like down her arm.

The girl's painted face contorted in pain, and catching Nell's eyes on her, she glared narrowly. "What're you lookin' at?"

Nell flushed to the roots of her mousy hair. "I … are you okay?"

"Do I look okay?" The girl winced and pressed her hand to her side. "Had an accident – *oh*! London … a bar … party … you know how it is."

Nell remained silent. The girl's eyes sifted over her appraisingly then she snorted derisively, "Well, maybe you don't."

Nell didn't respond. She returned to her book though the stranger's eyes rested heavily on her.

"Ever been overseas?"

Nell looked up, startled. "No." She said it with finality, almost turning away when something stopped her. "I'd like to go to Bali maybe, but … " she paused – she never conversed with strangers on the train.

"But what?"

Nell shrugged. "I don't know … no-one to go with, I suppose."

"So? You don't need someone to go with. Travel's amazin' – you might *go* alone, but you'll never *be* alone. I went on my own – great time. Even now … no regrets."

"You made friends there?" Nell said, feeling rather brave.

"Had friends already there. Met me at the airport and we … *aahh* … " the girl gasped, "had a ball."

Nell turned to watch the street lights flash past the window. Adjusting her focus, she saw her own reflection; uninspiring, matronly clothes, no make-up, bland hair. Dejectedly, she turned away to find the stranger watching intensely.

"My aunt's in London," Nell said flatly. "Mum's younger sister, but she's more my age. She's always inviting me over."

"There ya go!" the other girl said triumphantly. "What's stoppin' ya?"

Nell sighed ruefully. "My boss'll only give me two weeks off at a time."

"Where d'ya work?"

Nell told her and the girl made a derogeratory noise, "Handbags! So quit, why don't ya?"

There was a sudden burst of laughter from the budgies in the carriage and the stranger curled her lip contemptuously.

"Do you know them?" Nell asked.

The girl grimaced. "As if." She shimmied backwards bracing her back against the wall. "Every Friday ... they're dressed up ... goin' out. And what're *you* doin'?" She grinned sardonically. "Havin' fun are ya?"

The train drew alongside a platform and the girl painfully stood, and leaning against the back of her seat, edged her way to the aisle.

"You need a hand?" Nell said, automatically reaching out.

"Don't help me ..." the girl said through gritted teeth, "help yourself. *Gorn*, give the handbags the flick ... get to London. What 'ave ya got to lose?"

The electronic doors closed and she was gone.

———

It was Monday morning and Bill looked over his breakfast at his daughter. His two boys were gone for the day – one to his job as an apprentice butcher, the other to school – so, he was alone now with Nell. As he watched, she buttered her toast and his heart melted.

He'd raised his kids alone, these ten years and more, and he'd done well with the boys. But Nell was different – here, he was out of his depth. The girl's only feminine influence was his seventy-something mother – a sweet thing, if entirely out of step with the young of today. The result, in a brown woolen suit and high-collared cream polyester blouse, was seated opposite him. Nell had as much knowledge of the trappings of modern teenage girls as he – but there was one thing he knew. He smiled to himself – he had a surprise for her.

"How's work?" he said, casually.

"Okay," she replied. "We're starting stocktake so I'll probably get some overtime."

He sipped his coffee, nodding thoughtfully. "Still saving for a car?"

"I've saved nearly two and a half thousand," she said around a mouthful of toast.

"There's this blue Datsun in a car-yard near work," he said enthusiastically. "Looks in good nick. D'you want to come look at it? If you like it … you might end up buying your first car."

Nell gulped down the last of her toast and got up. "That'd be good, Dad. See ya tonight."

He waited for her customary wave through the window as she headed off to the station. *Yes*, he thought returning her salute, *wheels. Just what she needs to get her out and about.*

Mrs. Crandall turned from the glass display counter and peered imperiously over her bifocals. "Nell. The Windex!"

Nell closed the STAFF ONLY door and passed the bottle and rag to Mrs. Crandall, who made a great show of scrubbing a barely visible finger print from the counter. "Clean the glass means *clean the glass*." She dropped the cleaning products into Nell's hands and turned dismissively muttering, "Next I'll have to go behind you with the broom."

Returning the bottle and rag to their cupboard, a faint voice stole into Nell's brain, *What 'ave ya got to lose? Only a dumb job*, Nell thought. The door opened abruptly and Mrs. Crandall stood there. Nell fancied the older woman's twin set was the same shade of mauve as her rinsed hair.

"Take your lunch break early, Nell," she said.

"But it's only –"

Mrs. Crandall's eyes snapped. "I can tell the time! I'm lunching with a friend … you'll have to mind the shop while I'm out, so go now."

Nell nodded, hating her meekness.

Outside in the sunny street, the disembodied voice echoed

in her head, *What 'ave ya got to lose?* And rather than suppress it, Nell listened, and she wondered, and she paused …

She was standing on the footpath outside a travel agent. "Don't think – just walk in there," she said out loud.

Brendan was teasing Mitch about some girl who'd declined a date with him. Nell, twirling spaghetti around her fork, watched the easy camaraderie between her brothers. Deflecting the teasing to their father, Mitch said, "When are *you* gonna find a lady, Dad?"

"Yeah Dad," Brendan said, "Mitch's so hopeless – maybe she'll come with a daughter."

The three laughed, and as her brothers applied themselves to their meals, her father leaned toward her. "About that car … I could pick you up from work tomorrow … we could go see it."

Nell hesitated. She'd forgotten all about the car. "Dad," she began but Bill was excited.

"Reckon you'll like it. I checked it out quickly today … it's nice and –"

"Dad …" Nell said louder, and he sat back questioningly. "I can't buy the car."

"You've changed your mind?" Confusion creased his forehead.

"No, it's just … I've spent the money."

Mitch and Brendan looked up, mouths open, forks suspended mid-flight.

"Spent it – *all*?" their father said in amazement. "Two and a half *grand*?"

Nell nodded, a little smile tweaking her mouth. "Pretty much … " The three were surprised into attention, and when she spoke, her voice trembled with contained excitement. "I've bought an airline ticket. I'm going to London!"

———

What 'ave ya got to lose?

A quick phone call to an overjoyed Aunt Olive completed the arrangements. Olive was beside herself, insisting that she and Nell would have the best time ever. "And Nell," her voice, with the faintest Londoner accent, sobered, "drop the Auntie thing, will you? Makes me feel so old. Ooh, I can't wait … the fun we'll have!"

———

Mrs. Crandall's pencilled eyebrows shot up in disbelief as she read the single hand-written page. "You're resigning …?"

"London, Mrs. Crandall," Nell said, jauntily, "and I don't know when I'll be back."

———

Now on the plane, Nell stared nervously from the window, but still, a stranger's voice, strained with pain repeated, *What 'ave ya got to lose?*

"Nothing to lose," Nell said out loud. "But everything to gain."

———

The plane trip was thrilling. Nell loved every bit of it – even the food – and then, she arrived.

As she cleared customs and dragged her suitcase through the arrival gates, Nell was nearly jumping out of her skin with anticipation and trepidation mixed. After nearly ten years, would she even recognise Olive?

Despite the sea of eager faces, Nell saw her immediately – drawn to the short black bobbed haircut topped with a cheeky beret. The slim woman in tight leather pants and funky hot-pink top rushed forward and gathered her niece into a tight bear-hug.

In the London cab they took to Olive's Norbury flat, Olive chattered non-stop of the adventures Nell would have and the friends she would be introduced to. And as the streets of London flashed past, the voice in Nell's head said, *What 'ave ya got to lose?*

This time Nell replied, *Everything*, and then, *I'll start afresh.*

And finally, the voice quieted.

———

"A bottle party?" Nell repeated, uncertainly.

"Yes!" Olive said, and her grey eyes sparkled. "Everyone invited brings a bottle of something. It's great … you'll get to meet all my friends in one go."

The party was arranged for the following weekend, and the days between were spent exploring the sights, sounds, and smells of London.

It was fast, bright, and throbbing. The streets, gasping with smog-pumping vehicles, were choked with people of every colour and creed. It was a contradiction between the old and the new, a confusion of roadways and a tangle of grotty, rubbish lined lanes. And Nell, brought suddenly to shiny-eyed life, loved every pulsing second of it.

For Olive however, was the realisation that Nell had missed so much that life could offer a young woman. She watched the expressions of wonder and delight cross her niece's face and pursed her lips thoughtfully. *Nell could be quite attractive really. I'll just bet Mario could do wonders with that hair.*

And so, Nell met Mario. "Hairstylist extraordinaire," Olive announced with a flourish.

"A virgin head!" Mario squealed ecstatically. "With *everyone* colouring these days, Olly *sweetie* brings me a virgin!" With a flamboyant genuflection, he took up his scissors and comb and set to work cutting, colouring, blow-drying Nell's hair into a glorious, chestnut mane, shot through with gold highlights.

The next day they hit Oxford Street and Nell, with Olive's innate sense of style, populated her wardrobe with a marvellous selection of jeans, skirts, tops and shoes – straight from the pages of glossy magazines.

———

It was an entirely different Nell standing beside her aunt, a glass of Beaujolais in her hand, greeting the bottle-party guests with a confident smile. In straight-leg blue jeans, a classy black jumper, a slick of lippy and touch of mascara, her transformation was complete.

Everyone agreed; the bottle party was a raving success. Nell was invited to a night-club the following Friday, and plans were made for Nell and Olive to join a group on a long weekend in Paris.

Nell fell into bed that night, exhausted and enchanted, and in those soft, floaty moments just before sleep, she listened for the voice of the stranger. But there was only silence – and the spirited sounds of a city with no downtime.

"London ... " she slept with a smile on her face.

———

Bill and the boys received Nell's letters, initially weekly, but before long they arrived fortnightly, then monthly. At first they told tales of castles and towers, bustling streets and smoky four centuries-old pubs. But gradually, the sporadic missives introduced new, vibrant people and places – Mary and Carol in York, Jeff, Liz and Margie in Edinburgh. A postcard arrived from Paris, and Bill's birthday card came from Amsterdam.

Bill wrote to his daughter. Though pleased she was having a great time, he hoped she wasn't living on her aunt's charity.

The reply, a month later, had Bill sit back in his chair, shaking his head in wonderment, re-reading the line, "Don't worry about money, Dad. A friend got me this really great job pulling beers in a pub in Earl's Court ..."

––––––––

So here he was, two years later, amidst the expectant arrivals crowd at Tullamarine. Bill's eyes scanned each person coming through the customs doors but he couldn't see her. He frowned as he fished her letter from his pocket – he'd not mistaken the details, so, where was she? Perhaps she'd missed her flight –

"Dad?"

Turning toward the voice, his mouth opened and the letter slipped from his hand unnoticed.

"Nell?" he said, in disbelief.

The modern and very self-possessed young woman standing before him nodded and threw herself into his arms.

In the car, Bill's eyes kept sliding to his daughter as she regaled him with cheerful anecdotes of friends and experiences, and his heart swelled with pride and pleasure.

Still smiling, he pulled into the driveway and shut down the engine. Turning to her, his eyes twinkled mischievously, "So, I saw this cute MG for sale. Reckon you might be interested in a look?"

Irises from yesterday

The photo-frame was wrought silver, heavy and old. In sepia, a man against a shrubbery backdrop, was captured mid-laugh. Pointing to something just outside the range of the camera, he turned as the shutter clicked, and a magic moment was frozen in time.

A lead-cut crystal flute with a single yellow-tongued purple iris sat beside the photo-frame and silently released a petal onto an antique lace doily, its faded fragrance made no attempt to compete with the tang of old urine and new disinfectant.

Propped against the vase was a colourised postcard of Our Lady. Its edges were scuffed and her blue robes had paled over time. The gold inscription at the card's base, *Peace Be With You*, was barely legible.

A hand extended, its tissue-thin skin ridged with corded, blue-veined topography, trembled and reached, claw-like toward the photo, but fell short.

Mavis sighed; a creaking sound that escaped through drawn-in, dry lips, and she squinted in an attempt to see the man in the photo. A vivid memory completed details her opaque grey eyes could no longer identify, for he was etched on her heart, this man, who had been taken from her ten years ago.

"Alright there Mavis, love?" A woman in a pale green uniform was standing in the doorway. "You warm enough?"

Mavis didn't respond.

The nurse approached. "Come on dear, let's get you to the dining room. Cook's made shepherd's pie." Her arm eased around Mavis' shoulders, her free hand touched Mavis' knee where the bone was lumpy under the fleecy, pink track-pants.

Mavis resisted with surprising strength and the nurse paused momentarily before trying again. "Don't you like shepherd's pie? And we've got jelly and custard for afters – now, I *know* you like jelly and custard," she said brightly.

Cheryl was exhausted and her back was killing her but she needed to get Mavis to the dining room for her meal. The old woman was wasting away and Cheryl, her emotions numbed from her years in nursing, attempted to view the situation philosophically; *We're all going to go someday, but at least when they're in here, we can ease their twilight.*

But Mavis had only been in the nursing home a few weeks and was sinking fast. Cheryl applied a little pressure behind Mavis' back, *"Upsadaisy,"* she said, but Mavis wouldn't budge, her face was turned to the photo on the little table and her eyes were misty.

Cheryl straightened, her hand unconsciously going to the small of her back. "This your husband?" she said, pointing to the man.

Mavis didn't answer, but her hand reached out and she sighed again. "Handsome in his day, wasn't he?" Cheryl said. She leaned over and picked up the photo, and was surprised by the weight in the frame. Mavis' eyes followed urgently, her fingers moving in her lap like talons.

Cheryl squatted beside the old woman and placed the frame in her questing hand. The claws curled around the photograph and Mavis pressed it to her sunken bosom. Her wet eyes sought Cheryl's in silent gratitude.

"What was his name?" Cheryl asked, forcing down the sadness that rose in her.

Mavis' mouth opened and Cheryl didn't flinch at the old woman's stale breath. The voice, when it came, was dry and delicate, like old parchment. "Ed ... mund."

"Edmund," Cheryl repeated, smiling. "A gentleman's name." She dragged herself to her feet. "Well, we can take Edmund to the dining room with us if you want."

Mavis turned her gaze to the photo without response. Cheryl decided to try again. "Aren't you hungry? Wanna go have some tea?"

At a soft noise from the door, Cheryl turned. Judy was standing there, folded arms resting on her chunky belly. "Couldn't get her to move yesterday either," she said ruefully.

"Perhaps I'll bring her meal on a tray," Cheryl said, "she can eat in her room."

Judy nodded. "Yeah we did that yesterday. How are you today, Mavis?" Judy said coming forward. Mavis' lips grimaced in a toothless smile and her half-closed eyes focused on a place in the past.

"Ed ... mund ..." the word escaped as a whisper and the two nurses looked to each other.

"I'll get a tray," Judy volunteered decisively.

"Tell me about Edmund, Mavis," Cheryl said, sitting on the edge of Mavis' bed. She pointed to the photograph, "What was he like?"

Cheryl watched as Mavis' eyes drifted out of focus. "Ed ... mund ..." Mavis smiled again and a single tear spilled into the crease beneath her eye.

The room was silent but for Mavis' raspy breathing. From

the communal dining room up the corridor, the evening meal smelled warm and inviting, and the sounds of clinking crockery carried abstractedly into Mavis' room.

"Ed … mund," Mavis sighed.

"What about Edmund?" Cheryl asked, distractedly casting a professional eye about the little room to ensure everything was in its place – nothing needed tidying.

Mavis weakly raised an arm and pointed a skeletal finger at the door. "Oh … Ed … mund," she breathed.

As the smile spread across Mavis' face, her features were transformed and Cheryl was afforded a brief glimpse into the past; a young woman's smooth-faced, welcoming smile, the love glistening in her hazel eyes. Comely Mavis had never been considered a beauty, but the face she turned to her man read clearly of a woman confident in her love.

"He comes …" Mavis whispered, and Cheryl, the back of her neck tingling, resisted the urge to glance over her shoulder, as if the elderly man was indeed standing beneath the lintel.

Cheryl watched as Mavis wilted, her eyes filled with unshed tears and she exhaled a shallow breath. "Gone … not time … not yet."

Cheryl's brow furrowed slightly, "Who's gone, love?"

"Ed … mund …" Mavis breathed sadly.

"Yes, Edmund's gone. How long ago now? Ten years?"

"She reckons he visits her." Cheryl started at Judy's voice behind her. The other nurse came into the room carrying a tray and Cheryl smelled the rich, meaty fragrance of the shepherd's pie. There was a serve of jelly and custard, as well as some orange juice in a spill-proof plastic cup. "Brings you flowers, doesn't he Mavis, eh?"

Mavis nodded and a secret smile tugged at her toothless mouth, "Irises … always grew 'em … in our garden."

"Gonna have some tea, Mavis?" Judy asked. She placed the tray on a wheelie table and dragged it closer to the old lady. "Ever since she got here, she's been saying her husband visits her room – don't ya Mavis. Told Nathan Edmund was going to take you away."

Cheryl gave an involuntary shiver. "That's kinda creepy," she said softly and Judy shrugged.

"Pretty much. Nathan said the other night he heard Mavis talking – figures she's talking in her sleep, so he comes in to check on her and she's sitting up in bed, chatting on like nobody's business. Gave Nat the willies, you did Mavis, teasing him like that."

"Ed … mund … comes here …" Mavis said hoarsely, and the two women looked at her. The ancient face was split in a gaping smile and she was nodding. "Here …" she repeated assertively, "with irises."

Judy shrugged again. "See?" she said to Cheryl. "Now Mavis, you know Edmund's not here," she patted the old lady's arm pacifically. "Edmund is –"

"Here …" Mavis said insistently, "Ed … mund comes … brings irises …"

Judy rolled her eyes at Cheryl and leaned forward and whispered conspiratorially, "Someone must've brought in some flowers for her that day, 'cause Nat said she had an iris in her hands." She shrugged and straightened. "I dunno … I got work to do. Mavis, you tell Cheryl all about it."

Cheryl and Mavis watched the nurse's wide backside swing out of the room before turning to each other. The older woman's eyes were wide and pleading.

"Ed … mund … loves me … will take me … with him," Mavis said and her breath was coming in quick shallow gasps.

"Where's he taking you, love?" Cheryl asked. Pulling the table closer to Mavis, she took up the spoon and dipped it into the shepherd's pie.

"With him … but he says … not my turn … not yet … but soon …" Mavis said, and submissively accepted a small spoon of mashed potato. Cheryl watched as Mavis' jaw moved up and down – the habit of a lifetime – on the food. Finally, she swallowed.

"Ready?" Cheryl asked, a second spoonful hovering patiently. Mavis nodded and held her mouth open like an obedient child.

Some time later, Mavis had only been able to do justice to half her shepherd's pie, but her eyes were heavy lidded and her chin dropped toward her chest. Cheryl moved the food away and standing upright, she stretched her frozen muscles and heard her back crack.

Sighing, she looked to where the elderly lady dozed in her chair. Cheryl moved to the wardrobe and, opening the door, took down a crocheted rug. She shook it out and tucked it around Mavis' knees. Even in sleep the old lady clutched the photo of her Edmund.

Cheryl smiled wanly and wondered if, like everything else these days, love just wasn't made like it used to be. Her own marriage would not see out the year, let alone a lifetime.

She placed the emergency buzzer on its extendable cord on Mavis' lap and picking up the tray, left the little room.

———

The halls were still and dark; the only light came from the desk lamp at the nurse's station and the nightlights at intervals along the skirting-boards that lent crevices and nooks for shadows to lurk. The nursing home hummed with monitoring equipment and, in the depth of night, seemed to have a throbbing, electronic life of its own.

Cheryl sat alone at the desk, a back-copy of *Reader's Digest* open in front of her. She generally didn't do nights, but with no-one to go home to these days, she'd volunteered when Margaret phoned in sick.

Suddenly she tensed, aware of a presence behind her. Abruptly swiveling her chair around, she startled Nathan with a cup of steaming *Cup-a-Soup* in each hand.

"Chicken noodle," he said, handing her one. "Mum said it'd put hairs on my chest," he affected a horrified expression, "I thank the sweet lord daily she got *that* one wrong."

Cheryl chuckled and took the cup he offered. "How come you always do nights? Don't you find it a bit lonely?"

Nathan took a sip of his soup, "Ooh, that's hot," he lisped effeminately. "I like it at night. Can be a bit creepy, but. And if I get bored I watch movie trailers on the 'net or catch up on my homework."

"Homework?"

"Medical stuff. I go to school three days a week and study at night. I'm gonna be a nurse – I think."

Cheryl sipped her soup, letting the artificial chicken flavour warm her insides. "So not much goes on at night then?"

Nathan shook his head. "I do the rounds a couple of times just to check on 'em, but generally the only thing that goes bump is Bert. Nice old chap, but prone to wandering around at night. Climbs into people's beds – doesn't do anything – but it scares the livin' daylights out of the old girls. If you find him, just lead him back to his room – docile as anything, he is, poor old chap."

Cheryl dipped a teaspoon into her soup to scoop the last of the noodles from the bottom of her mug.

"Here," Nathan held out his hand. "Give's your cup. I'll take it to the kitchen and check on the west wing on my way. Can you do the east?"

Cheryl nodded, grateful for something to do. She watched as Nathan disappeared down the hall before getting up from her chair and heading in the opposite direction.

The corridor was wide with doors opening off both sides. Cheryl decided to walk down the left, checking all the rooms on that side until she reached the end, then she'd turn and check all the rooms on the other side on her return.

Each room was dimly lit by a comforting glow filtering through a vent near the floor. It allowed Cheryl enough light to check the occupants were comfortable in their beds. At Mavis' door, Cheryl paused – the lady looked small and peaceful, smiling vaguely in her sleep – before moving on.

Finally, she arrived at the great glass window looking onto a small courtyard at the end of the hallway. Outside, a callistemon stood silently on the left, a lemon tree, drooping under the weight of bulbous fruit, was on the right, and directly in front, gilded by a sliver of moon, was a wrought iron table with two chairs.

Cheryl stood staring outside for a moment more until a prickling at the back of her neck caused her to turn around.

"Bert!" It came out like a stage-whisper in the darkness. The silhouette halfway up the corridor ignored her. "Bert?" Cheryl said a bit louder as she started toward him. The man was standing in the gloomy hall and Cheryl strained her eyes to see him, but it was difficult through the dimness.

As she drew closer, he turned into one of the rooms and disappeared – Mavis' room.

Cheryl made a *tutting* sound to herself. So this was why

Mavis thought Edmund was visiting her. All she needed now was for the old dear to waken with a fright.

Mavis' door was slightly ajar, as Cheryl had left it. She pushed it further open and went inside. There was no sign of Bert. She looked behind the door – nothing, then went carefully around the bed in case he was hiding in the shadows – still nothing.

"Bert?" Cheryl said softly. "Come on love, let's get you back to bed."

The room was strangely silent, not even Mavis' breathing broke the peace, but Cheryl didn't give it a thought, she was becoming confused. Perhaps he was in the ensuite.

She pushed the door to the bathroom and felt the emptiness within as the door swung open on smooth, soundless hinges.

"Bert ..." She said it in her normal voice now, growing slightly irritated. She could have sworn Bert came into this room, though perhaps the dark had deceived her. Maybe he'd gone into Glad's room next-door.

As she turned to leave, her eyes made a last sweep of the room, and something caught her attention. She moved closer to the bed, squinting through the dark to be sure she wasn't mistaken – and she wasn't.

"Oh, dear," Cheryl murmured sadly, and reached for the bed-side lamp. Clicking it on, an arc of light was thrown across the room, illuminating the woman in the bed.

Mavis' aged cheeks were smooth and slightly pinked, and the soft lips curved in a contented smile. In her final, endless sleep, the last decade of loss and grief had fallen away to reveal Mavis as Edmund would have known her.

On the pillow, beside her face one white hand rested on a fresh purple iris, the dew still clinging to the lush green foliage.

Kay's café

Oh hi. Is that Kay's café?

Yes, it is.

Could I place an order please?

What would you like, love?

Er, a cheese and tomato toastie, with pepper, no salt.

Yes …?

And a black tea.

Your usual table? By the window?

Is the sun coming in?

No. The blind's down. It's a stinker today.

Lucky you. We wouldn't know summer was coming down here. So how've you been, Grandma?

Oh you know … usual back-ache, but not bad. Doctor's got me on these new pills. Reckons it'll ease the pain but I dunno. Nothing seems to work at my age. Anyway, where are you?

At work. Guess what … My exam's coming up next week. A biggie – counts for half my score, but it's the last one for the year – thank heavens.

It's only October. We never finished school this early in my day.

This is uni. It's different.

Anyway, you'll do well. I always said you got your brains from your grandfather. Funny your mother never got any – behind the door when they handed out brains. Still with that bloke?

Suppose so, haven't heard from her in ages – was that the doorbell?

It'll be Mavis.

You should've said. I wouldn't have kept you.

I'd rather talk to you – hang on – *Just a sec, Mavis*.

You'd better go Grandma –

I'd better go love. I'll call you next week.

Love you …

Love you too …

———

Bren love, it's Grandma. Sweet Mary I hate talking on these things they're so … mechanical. Well … you're not there so … call me when you get a chance. Just wanted to know how you went on that exam, okay …? Well … alright … bye for now.

———

Is that Kay's Café?

Certainly is. I've got some nice ham this week
would you like some of that?

Yeah, with home-made pickles?

Usual table by the window?

You betcha! I got your message, Grandma.
Sorry I wasn't home – you'll never guess – you
remember that guy I told you about?

The one with the border-collie?

Yeah him. Well, the other day, I'm sitting in the
park studying and he goes past. But this time
he stops and guess what!

What?

He asks me for the time.

Oh … that's very encouraging.

It was cos I told him it was twelve-thirty and he
said, oh lunch-time. Can I buy you a sandwich?
So what about that? More than encouraging.
Jed was with him – the border-collie – so we
went to this café where we could sit outside,
and they brought a bowl of water for Jed and –

What's his name, love?

Greg – and he's twenty-eight, has his own
apartment, and works at some technology
company.

Sounds nice.

Don't you think?

As long as you're happy.

Grandma … you could sound pleased for me.

I'm just worried you'll rush things. Remember that last one broke your heart ... Just don't want you getting hurt again.

Yeah, but that was two years ago. Older and wiser now.

Oh dear! No matter how old we girls get, where men are concerned we're never wiser.

Cynic!

And I've had seventy years of experience to get this way.

Anyway I've got more news. I've got a mobile phone now. You can call me wherever I am and always get me.

No more machine?

Nope! Grab a pen – I'll give you the number.

Okay ... ready.

Oh-four-six-six ... one-two-three ... seven-six-seven. Got it? Okay ... Gotta go. Greg's coming over. Love you Grandma.

Love you too.

———

Hello?

Bren is that you?

Grandma! How are you?

Is this that mobile? Number seemed very long. I thought I'd written it wrong.

No, you got it right.

Where are you?

Driving home from work.

Did you have a good day?

Yeah … Grandma I gotta go. Don't have a handsfree, if the cops catch me …

Oh … sorry … I'll talk to you later.

Bye Grandma … love you!

Love you too.

———

Hello?

Bren?

Grandma … hi!

Brenda?

Grandma it's me!

Brenda … can you hear me? What's all that racket?

I'm at the pub with friends. I passed! Ninety-seven percent!

Well done dear!

Thanks Grandma. Look, I gotta go … Greg's about to make a speech. I'll ring tomorrow. Love you –

What …?

I said I'd call you tomorrow.

What about tomorrow? I can hardly hear you over the noise.

Tomorrow! *I'll … call … you*!

Alright. Have a good night.

Bye Grandma.

———

Hello?

Hi. Is that Kay's Café?

Oh Brenda, we're not open for business.

What? Grandma, what's wrong?

Well … a little accident, that's all. Nothing too –

Are you alright?

Tut. I'm a silly old woman, Bren. I crumbed some fish and was heating oil to cook it and forgot. I went out to water and heard someone's smoke alarm-thingy going off. It's funny really. Turns out it was *my* alarm.

How bad is it?

Just the kitchen. The insurance man is coming over tomorrow. S'pose he'll want to know all about it.

He probably will. Grandma, you're gonna have to be more careful.

Don't start on me Brenda. It could've been worse, I mean, only the other day …

What?

Never mind.

What?

Look, it's nothing. Anyway, you caught me reading *Pensioner's Weekly*. I'm in the middle of this article about incontinence. Must go.

Okay, Grandma.

Okay?

Love you, Grandma.

Love you too, dear.

———

Hello?

Hello dear.

Oh hi Grandma – oh that's nice, does it come in red?

What?

Sorry Grandma, I'm in a shop. They've got this great – er … no that's a bit pink, just a shade darker would be good – Greg's taking me to the Easter Cup and I'm looking for a dress – that's it! That's perfect. Can I try that one on?

Bren, I need to talk to you. I … I'm a bit …

Hang on Grandma – do you have it in twelve?

Bren, is this a bad time? I'll ring back.

What? Just a sec, Grandma – tens never fit across here. It has to be a twelve.

Brenda, I'll ring tomorrow.

Oh, that might be okay. Grandma, just a sec, will you?

Look, you're busy now. I'll speak to you later.

Grandma …? Hello …?

Hello?

Bren, it's Grandma.

Hi Grandma. How you doin'?

Oh, not too bad. I've got the new cupboards in the kitchen. Insurance paid for everything – looks nice too. Maybe the fire's going to be a good thing.

Hmmm. Don't make a habit of it.

Oh no … where are you? It's so noisy there.

We're at a restaurant. Greg won big at the Easter Cup. He's buying dinner.

Greg? Is this a new bloke?

What …? What are you talking about?

This Greg. You've never mentioned him before.

Um … Grandma? I've told you all about him.

You might've mentioned him, I don't know.

I … I've been seeing him for nearly eight months.

Honestly Brenda, I can't keep up with all the names you throw at me.

That's not fair, and it's not true …

…

So anyway, whatcha ringing for?

You don't have to be nasty, Brenda.

I'm not being nasty – I just asked why you rang.

Can't I ring when I want to?

Yeah, but I'm that busy right now.

Then it doesn't matter.

It obviously does. What is it?

Nothing. Anyway, you yelled at me and now I've forgotten.

Sorry Grandma. Look, how about I ring tomorrow … Grandma?

I suppose.

Alright. Put the kettle on at eleven and
we'll chat over a cuppa.

Okay.

Love you Grandma.

Love you too.

———

Hello?

Hello, am I speaking to Brenda?

Yes. Who's this?

It's Mavis – Kay's – Your grandma's friend.
We haven't spoken in a long time.

Er … no. How are you Mavis?

Oh I'm alright. Listen love, it's Kay. She's okay
but she's had a bit of a fall. In hospital at the
moment.

Is … did she hurt herself?

Little crack on the head but she's a tough old
bird. Look, it's not the fall. I wanted to have a
chat with you … your Grandma's not well,
Brenda. I think she's going a bit … you
know … dippy.

What do you mean dippy?

I don't want to frighten you, dear, but she's
getting very forgetful. Like that alzirers thing
or …

Alzheimers?

Hmmm. She's struggling a bit these days.
I think you ought to get up here and see her.

Yeah … she has been forgetful lately but … she *is* getting on. She's alright.

I don't know. Best you come up …

I'm flat out at the moment, Mavis. Work is –

Look Brenda, it's important. She didn't even know me the other day …

…

If she'd just had a fall she was probably confused.

No. Before the fall. I think –

When's she due out of hospital.

They're letting her out tomorrow.

Okay. I'll call her then and see how she is, alright?

I don't know …

It's the best I can do.

Then, that's it?

I'm just so busy Mavis. I'm sure she's alright.

Very well. If you say so.

Bye Mavis.

Alright Brenda.

––––

South Ward … can I help you?

Oh, hi. Could you put me through to Kay Palmer please?

Palmer … Kay … just a moment …

Hello?

Grandma?

Brenda?

Hi Grandma. How are you?

Alright I suppose.

Mavis told me you had a fall.

Mavis?

She rang me this morning. What happened
Grandma? Are you okay?

I had a fall.

Yes …

They tell me I was lucky. Coulda been worse.

You're going home tomorrow, is that right?

I suppose. They don't say much. Just keep
feeding me this mushy stuff and jelly for afters.
None of 'em know how to cook!

You should tell 'em about Kay's Café.

Kay's what? Can't hear you love – I'm very tired.

I'll let you go then. Get plenty of rest Grandma.
Love you.

Love you too Bren.

———

Hello?

Hello. Is that Kay's Café?

I'm sorry …?

Kay's Café – Is that Kay's Café?

Oh no dear, this isn't a Café. You must have the wrong number. Bye-bye.

Grandma …? Grandma!

––––––––

Hello?

Grandma!

Oh Brenda – I nearly didn't answer. Someone just rang asking for a Café – thought it was them again.

Grandma it was me. I asked for Kay's Café.

Now, why would you do that?

…

Brenda?

Sorry, I … I was … just being silly.

I don't understand you love. Anyway, what were you after Bren? I've got a tray of scones in the oven.

I wanted to see how you were.

I'm fine. Busy … don't know where the day goes. Your Grandfather, God keep his soul, used to have this joke about Italians –

Yeah, you've told me before. So you're home from hospital.

Hmmm … yesterday – no, Monday. Hyder-range
were desperate for water. And the weeds!
Spent the afternoon on my knees with a trowel.

Glad to be home though?

Nothing like your own bed.

Grandma, I was thinking. You haven't met
Greg yet. I thought we might drive up over the
Queen's Birthday long weekend and –

Who's Greg?

Ohhh.

Now don't sigh at me Brenda it's not my fault
I can't keep up.

Please let's not do this again – he's my boyfriend.
Maybe if you met him you'd remember.

Hang on a sec … I think something's burning …

Better check the scones.

Scones?

The scones! You've got scones in the oven,
haven't you?

Have I?

You said … Just go and check for God's sake
before you burn the kitchen down again.

Now Brenda! I don't know what's got into you
lately. You were never this rude.

Grandma *please* go and check the oven!

Good heavens! Why don't you call me back
when you're in a better mood!

Bye Grandma …

———

Hello?

Good afternoon. Am I speaking with Brenda Stone?

Yes. Who is this?

My name is Doctor Marjory James. I'm Kay Palmer's GP. You were listed as her next of kin.

Is everything alright? What's wrong? She's … she's –

She's alright. I've had her admitted to the Base Hospital. She's had a little … er problem. From what I've been told, she was at the supermarket this morning and became disoriented. The staff were very good … gave her a seat and a glass of water but she couldn't tell them where she lived. Fortunately she had one of my appointment cards in her bag and they phoned me.

What's going on, Doctor?

Miss Stone look, you must be aware that she's been deteriorating rather rapidly?

Um –

I'm having her assessed, but I need you to know … It's doubtful she can continue to live alone.

Then …?

So if the assessment results are as I expect, I'll be recommending she go into care.

…

Miss Stone …?

I'm here.

Do you understand what I'm saying? She's had
an awful lot of accidents lately – more than you
know – and from the state she's in … well, she
doesn't seem to be looking after herself very
well.

I didn't know.

Miss Stone, I understand you live interstate …?

Yes …

I think you need to make a trip. It'll be good for
her to see you and I have – depending on the
assessment of course – some paperwork I need
you to look at.

Okay …

Miss Stone … your grandmother is not a
well lady. She is strong, physically, but …

I'll come straight away. I'll talk to work …
I'll … I'll fly up tomorrow.

Good. Please call my office when you arrive.
I shall fit you in …

———

Can I help you, miss?

Yes … I'm here to see Kay Palmer

Palmer … Palmer … Mrs Palmer's on
South Ward, bed fourteen.

Thank you.

Grandma …?

Hmmm?

Grandma … it's me …

Brenda? Oh Brenda love … it's so good to
see you …

How are you Grandma?

Not bad … *ohhhh*.

That's a big sigh!

Well, I don't like it here. You know I don't like
hospitals.

I know … Look! I brought you some Turkish
delight – your favorite!

That's nice of you dear. Your grandfather ate the
last lot you brought me.

Grandad?

You know what he's like. All chocolate's fair
game with him. Anyway, you'll be seeing him
soon. He's coming to pick me up … in the new
car, no less!

New car?

Brand new! Nineteen sixty-five XP Falcon
something-or-other … not that I care … but he's
thrilled to the back teeth – straight off the
assembly-line, he reckons.

Oh …?

Now, what about you? Finished your
homework? I've told you before Brenda, there's
no going out to play until you've done your
homework.

Er … yes … maths. All finished.

Good … good. Now off you go … I'm very busy.
Gotta make tea.

Love you, Grandma.

Love you too, Bren.

———

Hello?

Brenda … how are you?

Oh Greg … I'm okay.

And how's your Grandma?

She's alright, but … It's horrible seeing her like
this. They put her in this nursing-home today.
It's nice but … it's hard being the only one to
remember how close we used to be.

I can imagine. So … what now?

I'm going to stay here … at Grandma's place,
even though it's difficult without her. I need to be
here for her. She deserves this much.

Hmmm, Jed misses you.

Just Jed?

No, not just Jed. That's why I thought we might
drive up to see you this weekend. The spring
weather is starting to kick in.

That would be … so good …

You crying?

No!

Whatever – I don't believe you though.

Greg … I'm ringing my boss today. I'm going
to resign. I've decided to stay here for a while …
at least until … until …

…

That's probably for the best.
I know.

…

So, what if … what if Jed and I moved up too?
You'd do that?
Why not?
Grandma's strong – we could be here for a
long time.
Good – make a real home together, eh?
You're serious?
Never more so. Anyway … this weekend?
You're on … drive safely.
Will do.
And Greg?
Yeah?
Call me when you're half-an-hour away.
Why?
So Kay's Café can take your order.
Kay's Café?
I'll tell you later.

The last goodbye

I love this church. I love the rough-cut bluestone and the roses crawling over the gate. They said it was built by convicts some hundred and fifty years ago. All the mourners are in black suits with dark sunnies, and they cluster in groups by the double wooden doors – and there's more arriving – some I haven't seen in years and in such numbers! *Hmmph* – didn't know they cared!

And there's the Jag pulling up – that's right George; make the big entrance. Is that another new suit? European? Only the best for you, eh? Still looking pleased with yourself too, but most people here know you for the arrogant twit you are. And Edie, how come you always look like you're sniffing a foul smell? You should've left him years ago. Now you're just like him.

Well, I won't be churlish about it, but I'd much rather you hadn't come with your phony bereavement. You had no regard for me while I was alive, you'll have sheer contempt for me now. Look at you both; too good to talk to anyone, swanning up the bordered walk like Lord and Lady Muck. I can pretty easily guess what you're saying with your heads bent together. It's so obvious the way both sets of eyes swivel in poor Janey's direction.

Oh Janey, my love, my dear, dear wife. How you weep, how it breaks my heart. I'm sorry, but I regret nothing. *Je ne regrette rien*. I hope they play that song. It was always one of my favorites – that or the Essendon Football Club theme song. Probably wouldn't recognise it now though, been so long since we won a game. Ha!

Whoops!

I wonder if they heard me laugh just then. No-one reacted. Mind you, there was that dog on the street yesterday … it had definitely looked at me …

Wow, I never realised how dark and cool this church is inside, and how it smells of wood and Mr. Sheen. And it's so peaceful with its coloured windows and big altar spread with that crisp white cloth. The beautiful chalices are gleaming and reflecting the candle-light. So restful. I'm glad Janey decided to have the funeral here.

And check it out; so many of them have come, just for me. The place is nearly full. Didn't have this good a turn-out at my twenty-first!

But poor Janey is leaning on her sister. They're coming right up to the front. She wants to touch the coffin and smell the flowers. She's murmuring something, and dripping big fat tears onto the footy jumper they've laid across the casket – my Bombers jumper! How cool!

Man, that jumper was something special. Got it signed by all the players after the ninety-three flag. Be worth a fair bit now, but Janey wouldn't know about that. George would though. She better not let him get his hands on it, greedy old prat.

She's clutching it to her heart but she makes this strange gasping noise as she pulls a face. "Holy macaroni that stinks!" She's laughing and crying, slightly hysterically.

"I'd forgotten ... he never let me wash it. Worried all the autographs would run out."

Sylvia's putting her arm around Janey's shoulders. "C'mon Sis, Father Mac's ready. We better get seated." She's leading Janey to their seats in the front row.

And there's Darren and Craig. Of course they'd be here, we were three of the best mates you'd ever find, right since the day we pulled on our first pair of boots together in junior footy. They're pretty cut up now though and Daz's talking, "... blasted egotistical, big-headed poser – no wonder Gil never had any time for him. Gil would've loved having the Bombers theme song played but *noooo*, George reckoned it was inappropriate – not suitable for a funeral."

"What's it to him anyway?" Craig voices my own question.

"He's paying for the wake an' all. Thinks it gives him the right."

Crap! I never thought of that. Poor Janey won't have two pennies to rub together until the insurance pays up. She doesn't know it yet but she's gonna be so much better off without me – and not just financially.

"Don't matter but," Daz was still speaking and I tuned in again. "I burnt it to the CD – first track – so hopefully Father Mac'll just hit the play button and away we go."

Craig chuckles, and I with him, but he quickly claps a hand over his mouth. *Aw guys, you have a laugh. You deserve it after all I put you through.*

Father Mac is starting the sermon and I'm suddenly beside Janey again. Seeing her up close like this, the purple shadows beneath her eyes and her sunken cheeks are so evident. She's screwing her hanky into a tight ball and her lips are pressed together. I feel a stab – my first – of real guilt.

"I just don't understand. Why did you do it?" Her voice is a thin thread – she's not really talking to anyone, but it's meant for me. "Oh God Gil, if you were so unhappy, why didn't you say something? I would've looked after you."

Well that's it. Now I feel *real* guilty. I draw closer, so close I can smell her favorite talc, but my words don't even stir her hair.

My poor Janey-girl, there was nothing you could have done. I couldn't tell you this but you know how they say that nothing is so bad that it can't be sorted out? Talk about it, they reckon. But I knew there was no help. I knew what the doctors were saying and I knew also that you would've cared for me, but to me … well, that was simply unacceptable. You ought to have a life.

Your friends will ask if there were any signs, if you knew what I'd planned. Of course there were no signs – as if I wanted you to know. That was my burden. Like living with my illness was my burden, until you took it all on board. And if you'd known I'd planned to do myself in – see I can say it – that would then have become your burden too. I couldn't let that happen.

So when they tell you, you should've known and you should've stopped me, they're wrong because I carefully ensured you didn't and couldn't.

But, my love, don't think I didn't try to live that way – I honestly did. There came a time though, when the weight of my failing body grew too heavy and I couldn't endure the grief, the pity I saw in your eyes every … single … day.

You deserve better.

And it doesn't pain me to admit this, but since that night when you found me, as you found me, the burden has lifted. If only you could know how well I am, and how at peace. And when you get over this, you will still have your life to live.

As for me, I have never felt as light, as liberated as I do now. If only –

Who the hell picked this song? George I suppose. I hated this song – it always depressed me. I only sang it that night at karaoke to take the piss. He's such a selfish old bigot, Janey-girl, make sure you stay well away from him. Don't accept his help for anything – he'll only throw it up to you for the rest of your life.

Father Mac is calling the pall-bearers. So, who got the gig? Craig and Daz – no surprise there. Cousin Neville – great kid! Not his fault his father's such a git. No wonder he was sitting miles away from him. Poor bloke has Edie's pinched look though, I've never noticed it before.

Tom, Ben, and Jackson, hmmm, probably Janey asked them – good choices.

But everyone is so solemn. I wish I could talk to them all; tell them how fantastic I'm feeling – no more illness, no more pain. My body is whole and functioning. It's just like the way it was when I was fit and healthy and winning the best and fairest. Shows how ill I was when you see how easily the lads shoulder my casket – I used to be such a big fella.

Okay, enough now. Everyone is standing and ... what's this brilliant light? It's amazing, like it's flooding through the open doors. Can't be the sun – too white for that and ... so blinding but ... serene, glorious. And it has this ... this pull, like a magnet. I know it's for me. I've heard that stuff about going into the light and I'm not afraid 'cos there's a shape ... a silhouette moving inside it that's strangely familiar. And ...

I can hear Janey sobbing and it's distracting me. A few others are crying too. Geeze, they're all so unhappy. But I'm okay, everyone!

There was so much pain, I hated my life and now I can jump and leap and sing like I hadn't been able to since I got sick. You saw me, you all watched me wasting away – you must understand! Please don't load yourselves down this way. I want to celebrate, and I want *you* to celebrate too!

Thank god that dreadful song is over but – hangon … Yeah, I might've known another dreadful George-selected dirge. No wonder you're all so unhappy filing out of the church with that rubbish playing.

This is too much! Where's that CD player? What was it Daz said – first track? I can do this. Patrick Swayze could do stuff in that movie, after a bit of practice. Nothin' to it but to do it!

The stop button first … oh this might … be … harder than … I …

Oh wow! I did it! They're all looking confused by the sudden silence so I better do this next bit quickly. Right – where's the play button?

Oh man! That's great! And even better – George looks really miffed! Wasn't too hard either. Hey, I can see some future for this trick. Good thing they can't hear how bad my singing voice is.

See the bombers fly up, up to win the premiership flag … Geeze it sounds great in the church with the accoustics and all.

And Janey's laughing. She's laughing and crying at the same time and the boys with my coffin on their shoulders are grinning and looking at each other. Daz and Craig look surprised; they're asking each other who did it? Ah, wouldn't it be nice if they figured out it was me?

But it's not that important, I'm just rapt they're all smiling – some are even singing along.

Whoops, here comes George hurrying up the aisle, looks like he's gonna have stern words with Father Mac. Bugger off George! Let's just apply a bit of pressure to the volume knob and … Damn, I'm gettin' good at this!

They're all boppin' along – including the ones that don't barrack for Essendon – that is everyone except George. He looks like he wants to throttle someone. Who cares, he never had any time for AFL; no shonky little earner in it for him.

And now they're all outside and I'm standing alone in the church. I can see them grouped together, framed by the great twin doors. They're loading the coffin into the hearse and some are laughing now and clapping each other's backs. That's more like it.

But wait-a-sec … that light again. So bright it's … It's like the colours of everything else around me are washing out. And so tranquil, flooding over everything, filling every space, even my lungs cos I'm now surrounded by this … this radiance! And the silhouette … It's … Oh it's …

Oh dad …

I'm coming home.

To love again

I sit alone in my darkened room, my cigarette
smoke spiraling upward to the ceiling, making
for me, my darling, a stairway to ascend,
and I can be in your arms once more.

I live with the memories of your laughter still
ringing in my ears, and my lips feel the gentle
brush of your finger-tips. How my heart pounds
at the very thought of the love we shared.
I won't believe you have gone from my life,
never to return through my open door.

All these years I have waited, my darling,
all these memories I have been longing to bring
back to reality. The tears and heartbreaks have
finally been rewarded for I have little time
left in this world.

And so my sweet, sweet darling,
at long last we can love again.

Robert Skepper

All that & everything

www.ingramcontent.com/pod-product-compliance
Lightning Source LLC
Chambersburg PA
CBHW070328120726
47909CB00008B/2647